# A RISING STAR

Candy Waring had two men in her life
. . . First there was her father, Robert
Waring, the famous actor of the British
theatre. A demanding man who was
determined to see Candy follow in his
footsteps. And then there was Ben. A
young, aspiring journalist who gave her
the tender, loving care she so needed, and
encouraged her to pursue her second love
— art. But then one day Ben left. And
Candy, crushed and lost, ran back to her
father's side to start a new life on the
stage. But Candy was also determined to
find Ben, even if it meant losing her new
life — and her father.

## Books by Suzanne Goodwin
## Published by The House of Ulverscroft:

THE WINTER SPRING
THE WINTER SISTERS
SISTERS
DAUGHTERS
WHILE THE MUSIC LASTS
THE DIFFERENCE
SHEER CHANCE

# SUZANNE GOODWIN

# A RISING STAR

*Complete and Unabridged*

# ULVERSCROFT
*Leicester*

Originally published 1968
under the title 'A Name In Lights'


First Large Print Edition
published 1999
by arrangement with
Severn House Publishers Limited
Surrey

British Library CIP Data

Goodwin, Suzanne
    A rising star.—Large print ed.—
    Ulverscroft large print series: romance
    1. Love stories
    2. Large type books
    I. Title II. Ebel, Suzanne. Name in lights
    823.9'14 [F]

    ISBN 0–7089–4106–0


Published by
F. A. Thorpe (Publishing) Ltd.
Anstey, Leicestershire
Set by Words & Graphics Ltd.
Anstey, Leicestershire
Printed and bound in Great Britain by
T. J. International Ltd., Padstow, Cornwall

This book is printed on acid-free paper

# 1

I heard my father's voice in my sleep. Beautifully-pitched, it had a cutting edge: an actor's voice. As I dragged myself awake I could hear the birds in the garden, the traffic in the distance. And the voice.

Undeterred by distance — my father was downstairs at the other end of the house — the voice rang. Like an athlete used to acrobatic leaps, it promptly leaped on me.

'And how, may I ask, can I be both in Athens and rehearsing at my theatre in London *at the same time?*'

There was a muttered reply from his secretary.

The voice rose in powerful derision:

'*The rest of the cast!* He cannot be serious! Does Silas imagine I am interested in the rest of his cast! Who brings the money into his box office, might I inquire? Silas has traumas. I am worried about him. Does he now imagine he is back in the forties at M.G.M., ill-treating Joan Crawford?'

Another muttered reply.

'Mrs. Brown!' thundered my father. 'Do not mention Silas's schedules! Ring him at once and tell him to tear them up.'

A moment went by and then I heard the bell as she picked up a telephone. It was a bad sign when Dad's secretaries dwindled into blind obedience.

I climbed out of bed and went to the window, and when I pulled open the curtains the sun outside was bright.

There had been rain in the night, and the Hampstead garden sparkled. Rose bushes were thick with buds and blooms; the syringa growing up the side of the house near the balcony was covered in flowers smelling of oranges.

Nature might riot as much as it liked. Indoors sounded like squally weather.

I pulled on a towelling dressing-gown which a friend in the wardrobe had made for me. Based on a costume design in *Julius Caesar*, it fastened on one shoulder with a silver shield. I enjoyed wearing the gown, and my sister Tamara enjoyed feeble jokes: 'How's the Senate?' or 'Give Pompey my love.'

I went quietly down the stairs. The house that had been our home for twenty years (in fact since my father had begun to be famous and rich) was enormous. Friends sometimes asked him if he would not prefer a more manageable place. A penthouse in a new London skyscraper, for example? He would listen, and then give his celebrated grimace, dropping his jaw and rolling his eyes so that whoever had spoken felt a perfect fool. His personality would never fit any house but a vast one.

My father expected his house to reflect contemporary taste, and every now and again some designer whose work caught his fancy would be commissioned to alter the look of the place. When this happened Tam and I complained loudly but my father ignored our distress, saying, 'Move with the times, move with the times,' as a wall was knocked down or banister removed. If we were not quick, our own treasured possessions disappeared overnight. Paint, carpets, furnishings, furniture were altered, the happy designer watching them go with a fanatic eye, sure that my father's taste and his were as one. So they were for the time being. Father was up to date in everything visual, from the designs of his productions to the clothes he — and his children — wore. But he was never avant-garde. He and the huge public who loved him thought the same: it was part of his power that he was exactly tuned to the present.

The décor just now was a stylised modern version of a Victorian ducal mansion. Walls were covered with silk, carpets garlanded with

3

flowers, paintings by minor masters (like many successful actors, my father bought pictures) were hung by gilded mirrors. There were rather too many marble tables topped with self-conscious flowers. The woman who did the flowers was afraid of Dad, and while working she nervously dropped carnations at his feet when he went by. He looked pleased.

It wasn't only the house which had become ducal. I had noticed my father becoming increasingly drawn to the role. This had started when he'd been knighted two years ago, and gradually he began to demand the service and awed respect accorded to last-century aristocracy. Always commanding, he grew tyrannical.

That morning I went barefoot across the hall as quietly as possible; as I did not want to risk meeting him I avoided the study and hurried through the dining-room. The duke's touch was particularly noticeable here: dark shiny furniture, bright shiny silver, and portraits of Dad glaring down as if he were already history.

I arrived at the kitchen door like someone who's arrived 'home' after hide-and-seek, pushed open the green baize door and slipped through it.

Harriet was making coffee and looking like a scientist in a laboratory. She used a glass percolator, glass measure and long glass spoon. This effect was enchanced by her white overall with long sleeves rolled to the elbow.

'Hi,' she said, not looking up.

I pulled up a stool.

'Dad sounds very spirited. What's been happening?'

'Don't ask me, Candida.'

'He was bellowing at Mrs. Brown again,' I observed.

'Sir has been up since half past six,' Harriet replied. 'At seven I was ordered to telephone Mrs. Brown and tell her to get herself a cab. He said she must have all correspondence finished before breakfast. There's a planning meeting to-day and he wants her to clear the decks.'

'How many decks has she got to clear?'

'From his face, I should think she's scrubbing the entire ship.' Harriet was quite unsympathetic. 'Mrs. Brown arrived ashen in the face, didn't answer when I offered her coffee, and went into his study balancing her letters like a conjurer with a damned great pile of plates.'

'Which she'll drop all over his feet,' I said. 'You might at least sound sorry for her. You'd be ashen in the face if you had that job and that treatment.'

'No, I wouldn't.' Harriet poured me some coffee. 'If you flinch, there's always someone waiting to sock you in the jaw. Men find it tempting. Particularly Sir. I don't know why she's afraid of him. I've told her time and again that he can't eat her.'

'But he can. He's done it heaps of times. He crunches up secretaries, bones and all.'

Harriet gave an unwilling smile. I had known her all my life. She rarely said a good word for my father, and waited on him as if he were Jehovah. Privately, to my sister and me, she had called him Sir years before he was knighted, occasionally replacing the name with Him or God. Her actual manner to him, though respectful, was salted with irony he was quite aware of. He combated this by exclaiming: 'There, I've hurt your feelings!' or 'Aren't I a brute, don't be upset!' He'd look at her hopefully but her impassive face didn't change. Watching these exchanges, I was never sure which of them was winning.

At forty-three Harriet had the muscley misshapen legs, short body and duck's waddle of the retired dancer. From under grey medieval hair cut in a bob, Harriet, haggard, yellowish, sad, looked out at the world.

Some unhappy tale had driven her from

the ballet to our family. She'd taken the job for a few months and stayed with us for twenty-three years. She'd seen my sister and me born, the death of our mother while we were still children, and Dad's rise to his legendary fame.

Harriet never sat with us, rarely agreed to have a drink with us, was occasionally coaxed into a chat. She came into the drawing-room only to announce a meal. Sometimes she reminded my father that he 'employed' her. That made him angry. She refused, by her personality, to allow us to love her.

I buttered some toast and asked her if she knew how Dad was this morning. How had last night's rehearsal gone?

'When Sir came home all he said was 'Ragged, and Edward Dobson isn't funny'.'

'But Teddy is funny.'

'Sir doesn't think so.'

'Poor old Teddy.' I'd seen my father with actors who were not giving him what he wanted. He treated them as he did secretaries, demanding more and more, never letting up. The few actors who survived because talent made them tough won his permanent admiration.

'He's an ogre, really,' I said, 'with bones bleaching outside his cave.'

Harriet didn't bother to answer. She was

laying a tray: all I saw was an enigmatic profile.

'How's Tam?' I asked, using the name for my sister that my father resisted. 'Shall I go up and wake her and ask how the rehearsal went?'

Harriet gave a very slight start.

'I shouldn't disturb her. She told me last night that as far as she was concerned, the rehearsal was absolutely fine.'

I was puzzled. Wasn't Harriet being a little odd? We both knew perfectly well that Tam was worried about her performance. It was scarcely likely to be 'absolutely fine' all of a sudden. Before I could say anything else, Harriet muttered disagreeably, 'Can't spend all morning jawing,' and went into the larder. Through the open door, all I could see was an uncommunicative white nylon back.

I watched that back pensively. I sometimes thought Harriet was a bit wedged in her role of ironic looker-on. It was like an actress's nightmare — condemned to perform the same part through eternity. The words and reactions of Harriet's role were pat, she had memorised them twenty years ago. They never seemed to come from her soul.

She came back from the larder, fetched the coffee percolator and the heavy tray, which she picked up with difficulty.

'*Don't* open the door for me, dear!' she snapped in the vinegary tones that only actresses know how to use, and only other theatre people do not mind.

Alone in the kitchen, I finished my breakfast. I was slightly intrigued. Why had Harriet looked startled when I mentioned my sister? Harriet always favoured Tam, who was the baby of the family, just eighteen. I thought it rather touching that Harriet continued to fight Tam's battles: my sister was tough and didn't need a champion. Perhaps the rehearsal had gone very badly indeed, and Harriet didn't want me bothering Tam with questions. My father at present was rehearsing his company, the Royalty, in a late nineteenth-century French farce by Jacques Ghilain. He was an author unknown to English audiences and Dad was hopeful the play might discover him for them. It was a ludicrous, heartless piece, of the kind that set the pattern for the best farce ever since. It was also to be Tam's real chance. Six months ago, Dad had given her a part in *A Midsummer Night's Dream*. Like many other pretty girls starting in the theatre, Tam played a fairy. She had one expressive little speech and she'd done that nicely. Most beginners would have. The farce was another matter, she now had a part that was one of the pivots of the plot. The part wasn't large, but it was funny. It needs technique to make people laugh: Tam and I were both nervous for her.

My thoughts depressed me, and when I'd washed up (which Harriet disliked me doing) I left the kitchen.

There was no sign of Harriet and no sound from my father as I walked gingerly along the main corridor past his study.

'Candida!'

The study door burst open, and there was my father, framed as in a huge photograph outside the theatre.

'Good,' he said, unsurprised at seeing me creeping barefoot down the corridor. 'I want you.'

How could he possibly have heard me? There was nothing to do but follow meekly, wishing I were fully dressed. Parents who thought of themselves as dukes did not approve of their women around the house in dressing-gowns.

Mrs. Brown scurried past, her arms full of papers. She was not allowed to get away.

'Mrs. Brown!'

'Yes, Sir Robert?' She stopped, almost with one foot in mid-air. My father's voice shot through Mrs. Brown like an arrow through some Saxon at the Battle of Hastings.

'Try to get Silas on the telephone again.

And kindly remember,' he said, holding up his hand, palm towards her, 'that the telephone is an instrument that needs intelligence. And co-ordination,' he cried as she dropped a sheaf of papers. She fell on her knees and scrabbled them together. I could just imagine her sigh of relief when she finally escaped to the safety of her own office.

My father strode across his study and turned to face me.

There was a timed pause.

He was forty-eight but in the brilliant light of morning he looked over fifty. His black hair was streaked with grey, his face heavy, in spite of vigilant slimming. He had the look of a sculptured Roman patrician in the Louvre. There was the same noble fleshy nose, broad high forehead, thick curling hair. You would know at once that he was an actor; he had the actor's high cheekbones, enormous lustrous eyes, the actor's big mouth, tough and tender. His was a face that, if you looked at it for too long, turned you to stone. He was Medusa. He did not turn your feelings or heart to stone, but your hopes. He ruined everybody else for you because he was universally lovable and haunting, and beautiful. Look on Robert Waring and you were hooked for good.

I had seen that power work in a theatre on

fifteen hundred people. And on one visitor who spoke to him for five minutes. He had been born with it. At first he'd been a talented handsome boy with the power just beginning to show. He'd nourished it and turned it into art. He knew perfectly well what his gift was and how strong his power. He had only to fix his victims with his brown eyes, or use his voice on them. They were helpless.

All except me. Was it because we were alike, he and I? Not in talent — never in that. But physically we were alike, my own girlish not-distinguished face oddly reflecting his. I understood him. I never had the slightest wish to dwindle into a slave.

This morning, having enjoyed roaring at Mrs. Brown, he was benevolent.

'I have to go to Athens on Friday to see Silas about the new motion picture,' he observed in a friendly voice.

'You can't, you're rehearsing the farce.'

'I can be there and back easily in twelve hours.'

'Dad. That kind of travelling throws you. It's bad for you. And you'll never be able to work the day after you get back.'

The radiant face darkened, a cloud passed over the sun. He detested hearing that he was ever tired, ever at a disadvantage.

I felt I had made the point. I decided to please him.

'How's the play going? Is it jelling?'

His thoughts switched immediately. The frown vanished, he began to walk round the room, talking about the play. Did I know how difficult it was to make farce work, keep it together? It was delicate, yet firm as rock. I had liked the play when I read it, hadn't I? He knew that I'd enjoyed it. But it was devilish difficult to pull it off. It was far, far tougher than comedy, and he would not have his actors turn into grotesques. It was too easy to coarsen farce. 'If just one member of the company doesn't get it right, the thing can fall to bits . . . ' I had no doubt that he was planning a horrible time for Teddy Dobson.

He moved round as he talked, and I hunched in a chair watching him. He had a loping walk that reminded me of a black panther I used to see in the zoo. His walk touched me with its muscular grace and lightness.

He stopped suddenly.

'What did I want you for? Mm?'

He gave me a sly look out of the corner of his eyes, and folded his arms. For a moment I wondered if the one subject we couldn't talk about was coming.

I braced myself as if waiting for a ten-foot wave.

Did he guess what I was thinking? He was quick to read the human face: it was Dad's book and he knew every page.

'Ah yes,' he said carelessly, 'two small things. Run upstairs and tell your sister I have moved the rehearsal from this afternoon to this morning. It's in an hour's time so she had better get up at once. We're rehearsing at eleven sharp.'

'Yes, Dad.' I gave a slight sigh of relief.

'And now tell me something,' he said airily. 'Give me your opinion of Mrs. Brown.'

'A nice woman.'

'Don't pretend to be a fool, girl, when you are no such thing. What do you think of her as My secretary? As the woman who works for Me?'

I didn't like the capital letters. Lately they were getting into a habit.

'She's efficient; intuitive; has a good memory,' I said, naming secretarial qualities my father knew perfectly well that Mrs. Brown possessed. 'I also think you're a fickle so-and-so. How many secretaries have you got through now?'

'What can you mean?' He stood in front of me, his handsome face innocent as a boy's.

'Fourteen,' I said. 'Harriet and I counted

14

them. And that doesn't include the long-haired one who never took off her coat because you sacked her before she had time. You're lucky they don't sue you.'

'Sue me?' he repeated, tickled.

'I would. I'd appear in court in beat-up old jeans and say you'd damaged my career. I'd make a speech about how the Tyrannical Star had given me a nervous breakdown. I'd break the judge's heart. And just think how you'd hate the publicity, everyone knowing what you're really like.'

'My dear child, your picture of me is flattering,' he said. 'The star tyrant, I like that. Yes, I like that. But it merely illustrates your childishly romantic attitude of mind. Comes from those corny books you're always reading. I pay the women well. I naturally want service. And intelligence. I would say I was a good employer. Possibly occasionally a slightly demanding one.'

'Dad!' I said. 'You frighten the poor things into their graves! Carole Brown was a sensible woman when she came to you at Christmas. She was a bit theatre-mad, but it's the mad ones who are willing to work all night. And you never pay overtime. She was good at her job. That man she used to work for in the film-production company, the one you stole her from, was heartbroken when she left. He gave her a silver tea-pot. Six months with you and she's a gibbering lunatic, dropping pencils and telephones. You're a bully. And anyway,' I added, 'the poor old dear's in love with you.'

My father wheeled round. He put his head on one side.

'Is she, by jove?'

'She's got seventeen photographs of you under the blotter,' I said. 'And I wouldn't add fuel to that blazing ego unless I thought there was a chance it might stop you packing her back to the film people, whom she'll bore nearly mad talking about you all the time.'

My father laughed. It always pleased him when women fell in love with him. He had the same manner when he won at games (and he always won).

'No, Dad, you be kind to her. Or I'll give her a couple of tips on how *not* to be afraid of you,' I said, getting up to go while he was still in a good temper.

'Don't you do any such thing. A little fear is healthy!' he exclaimed, just as Mrs. Brown came in, looking at him nervously over the top of a basketful of mail that would last a large manufacturing company for a week.

I went upstairs to wake my sister. Tamara had been named after one of my father's successes as I was. I was born when Dad was playing Marchbanks — he was a skyrocketing success — in Shaw's play. He had been twentyfour, handsome as the devil, and was already known for the quality that made people love him. Tamara was born in Hollywood three years later while he was making an epic about eighteenth-century Russia. He'd looked wonderfully romantic in furs, bowling along St. Petersburg streets in a sledge. 'Tamara' had been the name of the Russian heroine.

Everybody but Dad called my sister 'Tam': her short name suited my short sister. She was five foot two and detested it because being little was a disadvantage for an actress. She was also inclined to be plump, and dieted irregularly but savagely. Tam was pretty. She had a round face, a turned-up nose, hair the colour of marmalade. She had my father's wonderful eyes that looked as if the pupils were permanently enlarged with belladonna, and my father's desire to be centre-stage with the spotlight full on.

Although she claimed as much temperament as Dad, Tam was earthier than either my father or me. She made a lot of friends, enjoyed social occasions, was rather a busybody. She slept like a log, and every morning woke, bounding with energy and good resolves, and had to run all the way to the bus stop because she was late.

'Why can't I have a car?' she often wailed.

'Stuff and nonsense. Public transport. Travel by public transport. How are you going to learn your craft if you're never in a crowd?' demanded Dad, who bowled past in his large black Rolls while we waited for the bus.

I went down the passage from my room to Tam's. Our rooms were on the second floor, under the Edwardian skylight of stained glass patterned with birds and clouds.

I opened her door.

'Tam! Time to — '

The room was empty.

Daylight filled it, the bed under its white bedcover was untouched, the shabby old Teddy bear in its place on her pillow. There was face-powder scattered on the dressing-table, some trousers crumpled on a chair. Nothing else.

I ran down to the kitchen, two stairs at a time.

Harriet looked up as I burst in.

'Tam isn't upstairs!'

'I know.'

'What do you mean, you know! She hasn't slept in her bed. Where the hell is she?'

'Maybe she'll be back any moment,' Harriet said, determined not to pronounce judgment. I could have shaken her.

'For God's sake, Harriet, don't be a fool. Where is she? Is she all right? Dad's changed the rehearsal, it's in an hour's time. *Where is she?*'

'How should I know?'

I could have cried with vexation.

'You know something else, I can see in your face. Suppose Dad finds out she isn't here.'

Harriet said slowly, 'She was depressed last night. The rehearsal went badly. Sir told her to go to bed and get some sleep. She went to a party instead.'

'Who with?'

'Johnnie Buckingham.'

'Oh no!' I groaned. Buckingham, a nephew of our local doctor Christopher Laurie, was a boy my father detested. He'd told Tam she was not to go around with him. There had been quite a row.

'That's why Tam slipped off last night,' Harriet said. 'I tell you, Candida, I don't know where the party was or who was giving it. I was a bit shaken when I went into her room this morning. I've been hoping she'd slip in through the back door. I wanted to ring Dr. Laurie. Johnnie Buckingham often stays the night with him.'

'I know,' I interrupted. It irritated me when Harriet informed me about Tam's doings as

19

though I knew nothing about her. 'What happened?'

'I couldn't get through. Mrs. Brown's been using the telephone since dawn. I couldn't leave the house either and go to the doctor's. The Italian lot aren't yet here, and if I put my nose out of the house when they're not around, Sir is sure to ring.'

The Italian lot were a married couple and their cousin who worked in the house, and with whom Harriet waged inevitable war.

'I'll go to Dr. Laurie's. Perhaps he knows where they are. Or perhaps Johnnie's back without her.'

I dressed hurriedly and went out of the house through a french window into the garden. My father couldn't see the garden path from his study, and I ran quickly down to a gate which opened on to the street. The sun was hot, the smell of damp earth was rich. Along the road a gardener was cutting a privet hedge, and shiny leaves and scented white flowers lay dying on the pavement.

Dr. Laurie's house stood on the corner at the bottom of the hill. He had lived and worked there for forty years, and his figure in navy-blue overcoat and bowler hat with curly brim was part of the district. Like the mulberry trees in his garden, he was a local feature. New houses sprang up, their roofs shaped like azure tent awnings. Dr. Laurie in his big dusty house, the brass plate worn with years of too much plate polish, remained unchanged.

'And a pretty penny he makes playing that old family-quack role,' said my father. 'Eight guineas for telling me to inhale Friar's Balsam.'

Dr. Laurie, who had sparse crinkly hair and a dry crinkly face, was a man you could trust with your life. He had been my father's doctor for years, and managed him beautifully, knowing exactly at what point Dad's actor-hypochondria set in, and undismayed by it. He was a worldly old man and I often asked his advice. Now I rang the bell, confident that I would get it and it would be good.

A blonde in red trousers opened the door, holding a book in her hand. She was new. Home helps always were.

'May I see the doctor? It is urgent. My name is Waring.'

'Please to come in please.'

She smiled in the way of someone mystified or deaf, and took me into the waiting-room where I'd often hung about before. She nodded and disappeared, leaving me with the old Sunday colour supplements and the clock ticking loudly on the mantelpiece. Time went by and made a lot of noise doing it.

I couldn't sit still but roamed impatiently round the room, now and again saying aloud, 'Oh do hurry!' I began to be sure that the blonde hadn't understood me. Was that book in her hand *Sixty Steps to English Conversation*? She'd probably got to Step Two. London was full of front doors opened by girls to whom one might as well talk in Chinese. I was just going out of the room to ask again when a man walked in. It was not the doctor.

Seeing my dismayed face, he laughed.

'I've been trying to decipher what Hendrika was talking about.'

'Where's the doctor?' I asked baldly.

'Went off five minutes ago. Back at lunch-time or later. I'm a friend. What the Americans call a house-guest. Ben Nash. Surely you're Candida Waring?' he said, sociably grasping my hand.

'Do sit down,' he said. 'Can I help at all? There's a locum we can call up. You probably know him. Can I help?' he repeated, solicitously pulling forward a chair.

I did not sit down.

'But I want Dr. Laurie. Where's his first call?'

Ben Nash scratched his chin. 'It's no good us asking Hendrika. The only English word she knows is Yes. I tremble to think of her fate in our wicked town, don't you? We could look in the book and see where he's gone but he probably forgot to put it, or did one of those scrawls you can't read. I've been caught with them before. Don't you like the locum?' He was a man who didn't beat about the bush.

I did not answer at once, because I was wondering if I was making a drama over Tam. Why was I worried? My sister knew perfectly well how to look after herself. But could she cope with my father after she was missing from one of his rehearsals? That *was* something to worry about.

I felt irritable and helpless.

Ben Nash asked again, was someone ill? He looked at me with a friendly curiosity, easy as an Australian. He was tallish, heavily built, with thick fair hair and grey eyes in a fattish face. He looked humorous, tough and cheerful.

'Do tell me what the trouble is,' he said. 'You're very pale. Are you sure you shouldn't be in bed? I could drive you to the other doc, you know.'

'My sister didn't come home last night,' I said, almost involuntarily.

He glanced at me in surprise and then burst into a loud roar of laughter. I was furious, and pushed past him into the hall, hurrying to get away from the laugh.

He came after me.

'There, I've offended you, I am sorry, it was rude.' In his anxiety to stop me running away, he caught me by the arm. 'Do forgive me. Please don't go.'

When I turned he looked genuinely worried; it was the face of a man who couldn't bear to hurt people. I stopped being angry when I saw that face.

'My sister went out with Dr. Laurie's nephew.'

'Johnnie Buckingham. He's staying here too, I know him well. Where did they go?'

'That's it. I don't know. I came round to find out if Johnnie's back, or if Dr. Laurie knew their where-abouts — anything — '

'Wait a moment.'

He went up the stairs two at a time. Almost at once he came clattering back.

'Bed hasn't been slept in. We just thought he was sleeping late, he always does. Johnnie's usually dead till midday. I found this.'

He held out an invitation card, scrawled in pink and yellow poster paint.

'Muff is giving a party.
Pow!
You come too.'

Below was an address in Camden Town.

'I'll get a taxi,' I said.

'Rubbish. I'll drive you.'

'It isn't your problem,' I said gracelessly.

'So it isn't,' he said. 'Let's go.'

We went out into the street, and as we climbed into his car I saw the clock on the dashboard. 'She's due at my father's rehearsal in forty minutes. We'll *never* find her in time!'

Hearing my groan, Ben Nash looked as if he might start laughing again.

'What happens if she doesn't turn up?'

'No one ever doesn't turn up for my father,' I said.

★　★　★

He drove fast through streets deserted in the Sunday-morning sunshine and we were soon in the unkempt squares of Camden Town. Paint peeled from houses where carriage folk had once lived. Outside a block of flats someone had gone mad with newspaper which lay like dirty snowflakes for yards in every direction.

'What a horrible part of London,' I said gloomily.

'Lively sometimes. Quite a good group plays round here. And there's a Greek restaurant I know. But I did once rescue a cat

from a meths drinker in that garden over there. He was strangling it. He thought it was a wolf.'

'How disgusting.'

The road named on the invitation card was a crescent of Palladian houses falling to ruin. Windows were filthy, curtains rotting. Front doors were mysteriously split as if someone had started hacking at them with an axe, and had gone away as mysteriously, the job of destruction unfinished. On stone steps patterned with emerald moss were milk bottles coated with the grime of months. In front of one faded saxe-blue house stood Johnnie Buckingham's rickety car. Scrawled across the car doors was painted gaily, 'Australia here I come!'

'Johnnie's got a long way to go, hasn't he?' said Ben, slowing down. He switched off the engine and the street was quiet.

'I think I'll go in alone,' he said reflectively.

'Don't be stupid; of course I'm coming too.'

'Please yourself, I was just being gallant. Thought they might be plastered or freaked out and it would upset you.'

We went up the steps together. The house had no railings, and hollyhocks stood in broken brick and broken glass — where did they find earth to grow in? A torch

extinguisher two hundred years old hung on a decorated iron hoop over our heads.

'I shall go in first, anyway,' said Ben, walking firmly in front of me into the dark hole of the open door.

There was a gentle noise of wailing Asiatic music as we went into a huge carpetless room reeking of smoke and drink. On a divan by the wall, a girl lay fast asleep, covered by a man's overcoat. Another girl, wearing a tight striped yellow and black dress which made her look like a wasp, was lying in a chair nearby. She opened her eyes as we came in, stared at us, and closed them again. Beside her was a trestle table with at least sixty empty wine bottles, many stuck with burned-out candles.

Under a large grimy window by the record-player, two young men lay stretched on the floor, both wearing jeans and patched boots; they reminded me of soldiers in the American Civil War. The music stopped wailing and one of the boys groped and set the record playing again, filling the air with its sad unexpected chords.

I went over to the girl in the wasp dress.

'I'm looking for my sister,' I said, raising my voice. 'Short, reddish hair. She was with a boy called Buckingham. Have you seen them?'

No reaction.

I repeated my question, shouting. She opened her eyes with the indifference of someone exhausted or ill. Hours ago she had worn a lipstick with silver flecks in it, it still outlined her mouth. She sat without moving.

I imagined a shade of recognition in her face and I said again, 'Red hair;' adding 'Name's Tamara.'

'Tamara,' she said very slowly. 'Waring's daughter. Yeah. We saw her. Too much of her. Left hours ago. My God, my head.'

She shut her eyes.

Ben Nash was talking to the boys by the record-player. He came over to me, hands in his pockets.

'It's like rousing the dead. Resurrection day. We need a trumpet. Had any luck?'

'She says my sister has gone.'

'I'll bet she wasn't watching,' said Ben, looking sardonically at the girl, a wasp dead on the tea-table. 'Let's go and look round the house. Your sister may have dropped off when the booze ran out. Most of us do.'

The house smelt of cats, our feet boomed on bare floors. A ghostly staircase ran upwards, torn lino nailed on each tread. Ben Nash padded down the passage ahead of me, saying, 'Stick close, don't go off on your own.' He put his head into one room after another

saying, 'Empty . . . Empty . . . One man in his overcoat — dead or stoned, take your pick.' Then he stopped and sniffed. 'Do you smell bacon?'

The passage turned a corner and we found ourselves in a stone-floored kitchen with high windows. Crouched by a blackened cooker, wearing the white silk shift she'd bought for one of my father's film openings, was Tam.

I went over to her in one bound, relief making me furious.

'What the hell are you doing here?'

She turned round, her dress squashed and dirty, her hair on end, a man's handkerchief knotted round her neck as if she had a sore throat.

'What are *you* doing looking for me?' she said disagreeably.

'Dad's changed the rehearsal. It's twenty minutes from now!'

The wreck that was Tam suddenly sprang into life. She shoved away the frying-pan as if it burnt her.

'Have you got a car?'

'Yes, yes, Mr. Nash brought me, where's Johnnie — '

'To hell with Johnnie! Come on!' She rushed out of the kitchen.

Ben Nash handed me his car keys.

'Come back with them later. If I know

anything about Johnnie's car it won't go. Hurry!'

For a moment good manners and Father's rehearsal battled inside me. Father won.

Tam was on the pavement, dancing with impatience. In the bright sun I saw a wine stain right down her dress, one strap of her shoes torn, and just how dirty her face was.

'Oh come *on*!' she cried.

I drove as fast as I dared. I was angry with her all over again but there was no time to say so. When we came to the bottom of the hill I said, 'I'll drop you by the garden gate. Dad's sure to be waiting in the car at the front door. Wash and change. I wouldn't like to see his face if he saw you as you are.'

'How long have I got?' She leaned forward as if at a starting post — her nose upturned, hair hanging, face perky and peaked.

'You're late already,' I said nastily.

★ ★ ★

The chauffeur was at the wheel of the black Rolls, my father already seated at the back flicking through a script. He looked up and asked sourly:

'Where is your sister?'

'Sore throat. She nipped down to Dr. Laurie's. He's given her a gargle.'

His expression changed from disapproval to alarm. No member of his company was allowed to be ill.

I asked him a couple of time-filling questions. He did not bother to reply, but arched his eyebrows at me. He looked at the front door, tapped the car window with his fingers. His face grew blacker every second.

Just when the storm was going to break, Tam appeared, jaunty in white jeans.

'Sorry, Pops.' She hopped in beside him, clean, energetic and professional. It wasn't the squashed character I'd found in Camden Town.

'Don't do it again, miss.' He gestured and the car moved off. He didn't wave to me and nor did Tam.

# 2

Driving back to Camden Town was an anticlimax. All that had mattered until now had been finding Tam and shoving her to the rehearsal. In our family to miss a rehearsal was like a nun missing Sunday mass. Now she was safely on her way, I reflected over her all-night session with Johnnie Buckingham. I wasn't looking forward to lecturing her about it. She would jeer and call me 'Aunty.'

Why did I bother to play Aunty at all? It's true that she'd spent the night with a lot of drunks in a filthy house in a slum, and in the company of a boy my father disliked. But I knew Tam, and I was sure the evening was innocent enough. She'd probably shown off, she always did. She'd dance and flirt and at times be boring and at times funny. I didn't think she was going to bed with Johnnie Buckingham. Her affair at present was with the theatre.

I suppose I could tell her that behaving badly was the way to do bad work. She'd agree. Tam always agreed and apologised promptly, saying 'Yes, Aunty,' or, if she thought me right, 'I know. I know.' It was dismissive. That she defied my father by seeing Johnnie Buckingham was another problem. I rather liked Johnnie. But I hadn't liked the house, its senseless occupants, or the story of the methylated spirits drinkers. I could imagine the place visited by the police. Johnnie was the sort of silly original boy who'd find himself, to his surprise, in a scandal. And Tam, at eighteen, was a mixture of actress and silly showoff. She was rash for effect. That was a way of getting into a scandal too.

When I got back to the house in Camden Town the door was still ajar, but no music could be heard through it and when I went into the front room all the people had disappeared. So had the record-player and the bright pile of discs. Nothing remained but bottles and smell; and a hollow left by the people who had been there.

I went out into the gloomy passage.

'Mr. Nash!'

My voice echoed spookily. I was relieved when a cheerful male voice shouted: 'We're in the kitchen!'

Ben Nash, Johnnie Buckingham and the girl in the wasp dress were sitting on the kitchen table drinking coffee from tumblers. Tam's bacon was still untouched in the frying-pan just as she'd left it.

Ben Nash stood up when I came in. The other two just looked at me.

'Did you get there in time?' he asked.

'Only just.'

'Nevertheless it's a relief,' he said, looking at me and winking. 'Have some coffee. It's horrible.'

'It isn't bad. Have a swig of mine.' Johnnie Buckingham passed me his glass with a smile. I smiled back, then remembered I was annoyed with him.

There was a silence until Ben Nash announced that we'd better go. 'We're probably the last humans ever to cross the threshold. I'll bet the house is condemned. They'll arrive and pull it down on top of us if we're not quick.'

'That reminds me,' said Johnnie Buckingham, 'I want to take Lynne here to Highgate Cemetery. Let's go now, shall we, baby? We could breakfast on a tomb. Some of them are split right open and you can see the bones. Great.'

'The bones'll be there another day. You come home with us,' Ben Nash said easily.

Johnnie looked at Ben as if measuring him. Then he shrugged.

'Okay, okay. Let me say farewell, then.'

He took the girl in his arms and gave her a long sexy kiss. He might as well have been kissing a chair for all the reaction he got from her. When he came up for air she just stared. She didn't even blink.

Ben Nash watched the kiss with interest, arms folded.

'I should say love among the graves wouldn't have worked this morning. Let's go, shall we?'

Johnnie followed him meekly out of the kitchen. When I looked back, the girl was watching us. Little and squashed, she was a wasp who had come to a sticky end in the marmalade.

'I tell you, Candy, I never could get going with that chick,' whispered Johnnie to me. He climbed into Ben's car and collapsed in the back as if he hadn't a bone in his body.

Ben walked over to examine Johnnie's rejected old red saloon with its cheerful 'Australia!' on the doors and its front wheels on the pavement. He opened the bonnet, peered inside, looked through a window, tried the door handle. He came back shaking his head, like a vet who has just left a very sick horse.

'Poor old thing, it'll never make Melbourne. It won't make Hampstead either if you don't send for it. There's one comfort, it is safe. You'd have to pay good money to get someone to drag it away.'

'You're just jealous,' said Johnnie. 'My car's a collector's piece. Yours hasn't got a vase of real carnations in the back.'

He closed his eyes for a while.

We headed for home, with Johnnie hunched in the back. His corduroy suit had apparently also been his pyjamas for weeks, his face was as tired and dirty as Tam's. Round his neck was a chain with a big silver emblem that had once belonged to a Lord Mayor. The thing was his talisman. He opened his eyes, revived and began to chat. He talked all the way back to Hampstead, growing quite cheerful. Did we know he was putting on an art exhibition? He'd found a gallery in Shepherd Market — good, wasn't it? A woman he knew (she had a title but she didn't use it) was letting him have it free. She was an ace, wasn't she? We must come to the show's opening day. It would be the fun thing.

His voice was cheerful if a little wavering by the time we drew up at the doctor's house.

'Well, folks, I'm for bed. I need all my sleep to keep these gorgeous looks.'

Ben Nash, standing on the pavement beside him, shook his head. 'You're not kidding, of course.' The look and pitying tone were the same he'd used over the broken-down car and Johnnie immediately looked all

36

sad and squashed. As he went into the house, even his back was woebegone.

'One of that boy's more tiresome traits is making me feel mean,' Ben said. 'Shall you and I have a drink? We deserve one.'

Looking back, I don't know why I accepted that invitation, except perhaps that nobody interested or excited me just then. The men with whom I went about were in the theatre and they seemed to give me nothing but spirited, endless shop. I'd talked that shop all my life: it was beginning to depress me. This man, standing beside me in the sun, was a change.

We drove off together, and he talked, and I only half-listened, thinking how different he was from an actor. His appearance, for instance. An actor cares about the way he looks every waking moment: even if he is dirty it is on purpose. Ben looked like a man who only glances at himself in the glass once a day to shave and do his hair. Energy and enthusiasm radiated from him — not, as with actors, for his new role, his future, his prospects, but for the streets of Hampstead, old pubs, new houses, money, politics, painting. His high spirits were catching, and when he laughed at his own weak jokes I joined him.

We stopped at a pub in a cobbled alleyway.

There was a courtyard at the back, with pink geraniums in tubs. Ben Nash shook hands with the pub-keeper, chose a table in the sun, and told me the history of the pub, in the space of five minutes. He leaned back in a cane chair, drinking lager. He was as uncomplicated as a good-looking honey-coloured dog.

'I've been thinking about the Camden Town thing. The morning after always looks pretty ghoulish, but I shouldn't worry. I don't think your sister came to much harm,' he said, smiling guilelessly.

I replied that I had not been worried.

'Ah, well, you never know. I mean it can be pretty rough for a girl.'

'Mr. Nash, make up your mind.'

'Call me Ben. When you say Mr. Nash I just don't know it's me. I shall call you Candida.'

He talked about Johnnie Buckingham. He'd known him since he was a baby. He informed me that Johnnie was half-Yugoslav, something I'd known since Tam first met him, and he quoted Johnnie's favourite saying: 'My mother comes from Zagreb and I talk fluent Zag. She wants me to get a job as courier. That's a polite word for spy.'

I'd heard it before, but it didn't matter because I liked him.

38

I noticed that he asked me various questions. They reminded me of the questions children ask each other, collecting facts like the cards in 'Happy Families.' When I answered, he looked at me in a thoughtful, interested way, as if measuring my answers against some idea or other that he had about me. I wasn't used to that kind of look. Actors talk to an audience: perhaps only an intimate audience of one, but always aiming to amuse or horrify or fascinate. To win you. They certainly don't ask questions with careful curiosity, or listen as carefully. Ben studied me as if he were making a sketch of my face.

'Johnnie told me that Sir Robert doesn't approve of his running around with your sister.'

'My father probably thinks Tam should concentrate on her career,' I answered vaguely. I wasn't going to talk about Dad.

'And not get involved with half-Slav hangers-on who let her pay for the coffee.' The words could have been Dad's own, they had the authentic ring. It was hard not to laugh as I murmured 'No, no.'

Ben Nash said that he did not envy my father having two daughters to bring up — with no mother. Girls were an alarming responsibility. 'I'll bet he packed you off to boarding schools and finishing schools, so

39

that old dragons who knew what they were doing looked after you and ordered you around.'

'Why do you think that?'

'Women brought up in that way remind me of fruit grown on an orchard wall, well out of the east wind.'

I admitted that we had been to boarding school and that my father had sent me to Switzerland. Tam had avoided the finishing school after she had heard about it from me and had gone straight to drama school instead.

'What's wrong with being finished? I like the sound of it. It's got a nice old-fashioned feminine ring.'

'It's old-fashioned all right. Like finding yourself with a lot of left-over Manchus. The school was a hideous place, like one of those huge iced cakes you see in old photographs in bakers' shops. 'Gold Medal, Brussels, 1930.' There was an enormous garden and views of the lake of Geneva from all the bedrooms and each room was decorated in a different colour. 'Carla's having the pink and you can have the *bleu de ciel*.' We went in boats on the lake and had classes out of doors and one of the girls played the harp.'

'What nationalities were the girls? South Americans? Swedes?'

'How did you guess? And Americans and some Italians and Spanish. We used to have letter-writing classes. How to address a Cardinal, how to write a letter of condolence to an Ambassador, the correct precedence at dinners for thirty people! Everybody was stinking rich.'

'Including you.'

'Of course we're not rich!'

He laughed again, as he'd done when I first met him. The laugh made me wish I wasn't with him, it set my teeth on edge as the subject of money did. Whether we had money or not wasn't something one talked about in the theatre. People talked about their parts and sometimes about their salaries, and about TV fees and box office returns. That kind of money was interesting. Personal bank balances weren't, and we behaved as if they did not exist.

'The finishing school sounds bizarre,' he said, happily dropping the unpleasant subject of cash. 'It doesn't sound right for an actress unless she wanted to play a Henry James heroine. Didn't I read you acted last year with your father in New York?'

'Only for a short season. Three months.'

'Another actor in the Waring family. When am I going to see you act?'

'You won't. I don't act now.'

There had been a stream of questions all the morning and I now waited for the flood. Even incurious people asked me about this part of my life. I was used to fending them off but not to the feeling they aroused in me. It was still sharp and still surprising. But Ben Nash was looking at his watch, and he said: 'Hell, I have to get back to work. Will you forgive me if I drive you home now?'

When we arrived at the house he got out of the car and stood in the hot sun beside me, saying good-bye.

'We must meet again,' he said.

I thanked him for helping me find Tam.

'It was so good of you. I'm very grateful,' I said and meant it.

'I was glad of the chance. I'll have a word with Johnnie about seeing too much of your sister. You never know. He might listen.'

He put out his hand and clasped mine. His hand was warm and broad and I liked touching it.

I went out of the sun into the cool house. The sound of Mrs. Brown's typewriter clattered at the end of the corridor. It seemed years since Dad and I had talked about her this morning. As I walked up the stairs, one of the Italian lot, a dark girl called Ventura, smiled up at me as she was brushing the carpet. She smiled slowly, her face round and

42

serene, an angel in a church painting.

'Hallo, Miss Waring.'

'Hallo, Ventura.'

I recognised, with a pang, the ardent expression. It was a look I had seen before on the faces of people at first nights, on film sets, at rehearsals. That look was because I was my father's daughter. What had I done to deserve it, except to be born?

I had a bath and dressed, putting on a denim dress Tam disliked. 'What ridiculous gear,' she had said (Tam pronounced it 'ridikilus'). 'You don't look like Dad's daughter at all. You look like a rep actress playing Florence Nightingale.'

'When I'm painting I please myself.'

'Madness!' exclaimed Tam. 'Supposing someone called.'

It was a phrase of Tam's. Someone would be sure to call, and that someone would be a director.

Along the corridor from our bedrooms on the top floor of the house was the room that had once been our nursery. We had spent much of our childhood there, eating nursery teas, doing jigsaws of the 'Counties of England,' quarrelling and dressing up. The rocking horse still stood under the sloping window, and nearby was the nursery mat with its two pigs going to market. Tam used to make faces at the smaller stouter pig wearing a bonnet, because someone had said it looked like her. When designers moved in to alter the house, Tam and I always hid the horse and the mat, dragging them out when the coast was clear, and solemnly putting them back in their ancient places.

Last year I had turned the nursery into a studio. It made a good place for painting, it had a skylight, and as the house was built on a slope the windows overlooked the sky and the tops of the garden trees.

When I went to work in the studio, my father would speak to me in quotation marks.

'Off upstairs to your 'work'?' he would inquire. 'Sold anything yet?'

'Is that your only yardstick?'

'Mine and everybody else's.'

'And when will you accept it as real work, as a matter of interest?'

'When you've earned yourself two hundred pounds at your painting I may change my mind.'

It was obvious he thought I wouldn't earn half a crown.

Because of his discouragement and sarcasm, I worked extra hard at school, and when term ended, I drew and painted for hours.

I wasn't particularly happy when I was

painting, because I wasn't sure I had much talent and I didn't seem to improve. My teachers said, 'Work, work, work.' I wasn't afraid to work hard. I was afraid of something very different, of the thing that Ben Nash had unwittingly touched on this morning. Some day soon the moment would come. My father and I would face each other and talk again about the thing I was frightened of.

Acting.

It was acting.

My father was determined to turn me back into an actress, and I was as determined that he shouldn't.

Like almost every other actor's child, I'd acted when I was very young. I had walked on in a production of my father's when I was five years old. It had been *As You Like It* with my father playing Orlando. For fun I had been allowed to appear on the first night, dressed as a page in the Forest of Arden. There had been sentimental photographs of Dad with me in the newspapers. Tam had cuttings of them in her scrap-book.

At school I had won acting prizes, which had surprised nobody, including myself. When I went to Switzerland my father had arranged for me to have a special course of lessons on '*Le Drame*', and coaching in voice-production. I had also been made to study the history of the European theatre. He had trained me like a race-horse. I liked it.

I came back to England and was sent to drama school, where I was 'the Waring girl,' received with a jealous friendliness. I went on learning and began to enjoy it. It was odd and satisfying to learn to act, to mix discipline and freedom, to use yourself and the world around you.

I had been at drama school two years when my father arranged to take one of his successes to Broadway. It was a new English poet's version of Racine, and had been a great success in London. The public until now had found rhyming couplets exhausting and seventeenth-century French art mannered. But this version for some reason caught the audience's imagination. It was the first time the English had enjoyed Racine for three hundred years.

The production became a British show-piece and was booked for a limited season in New York; a small but important part, that of a Greek princess, fell vacant. My father gave it to me.

It was an alarming first chance for a student, but I was excited and not at all frightened. It was fun to be surrounded by drama-school friends, encouraging and admiring and envious. Of course I would do well. Wasn't I lucky? Wouldn't they give their eye-teeth to have a jewel of a part like that, and to play in New York with Sir! (Harriet's nickname was now universal.)

Sanguine, cheerful, I flew off with the company.

From the opening until the play closed thirteen weeks later was a nightmare.

I could not act. I simply could not do it. My girlish grip of the art, the things that I'd started to learn, slipped away as if I had never known them. I spoke the part, went through the motions; I was like a wooden doll.

Actors have warm hearts, and one or two members of the company were touchingly kind. My father, they said, had that effect on beginners. He towered over people.

'Stop having nerves and wondering what he's thinking,' they counselled. 'Act. Go on. Just do it. Forget him.'

Forget him? — when, each performance, dressed in ruddy Grecian robes and crowned in laurel, his face scarred and beautiful as a god, he staggered across the stage, his arms outstretched towards me.

It might seem that to act with one of the greatest actors in the world would make even a small talent begin to flower. But when I was on stage with my father, close to his enormous art, I was numb. It was as if brain, personality, the way I moved and spoke and looked, became frozen. Off stage, I was a living breathing girl; on stage I was like a fern imprisoned in a lump of ice on the fishmonger's slab. Once, just before the first night, he took me out to supper and talked to me about my part, painstakingly explaining things to me, encouraging me. And then, when the run started, he dropped me. We were never alone. We scarcely exchanged a word until we returned to London.

We sailed home because my father wanted 'a few days off, for heaven's sake.' On board ship I was walking on deck one bitter cold morning — it was December — when Father appeared. He was wearing a chunky scarlet sweater and sparkling with vitality. He seized my arm.

'Come along. We'll play deck tennis and I'll beat you, Candy!'

He hadn't used that name for months.

★ ★ ★

When we were home again I finished my course at drama school (there were only six more months to go) but I was no good any more, however patient the teachers were, and they knew I'd lost more than my nerve.

'Perhaps I never was any good,' I said to

48

the principal on the day I left.

He was one of my father's friends, and he said earnestly: 'Rubbish, rubbish, I've heard that tale before! Some of my best actors have left these portals in tears! You need rep. A year in rep.'

But I took a bus down the street to the nearest art school, and used my mother's name to enrol: 'C. Shelbourne.'

'What's the C. for?' said a dark boy at the next easel.

'Candy.'

'I like that. Sweet as Sugar Candy. You're not bad at still life. Let's have lunch.'

That was how I escaped from the theatre.

★ ★ ★

The sun had moved and was slanting through the window on the right of the studio, lighting up the rocking horse's blood-red nostrils, when Harriet came in with lunch.

'Sorry I'm late. I had to take sandwiches down to the rehearsal for Sir.'

'How was it going?'

'Teddy's still getting it hot and strong. Brother, I wouldn't like to be in his shoes,' she said pouring some orange juice. 'When I came in, Sir was standing looking the poor slob up and down, and saying, 'Be funny,

Dobson, be funny." She glanced towards my drawing board and asked if she could look.

I was working at a still life, a pair of gloves and a pheasant's feather. I had chosen the gloves because the leather was pitted, and the creases made from my father's hands made them touching and evocative. The feather was contrasting, shiny and speckled.

Harriet narrowed her eyes as she looked at the sketch and murmured that my mother would have liked to see it, she had been able to draw, too.

When Harriet talked about my mother, her face lost its irony: it managed to look almost tender. I wished she would sometimes look at me like that but she never did.

'Your mother only sketched a bit, you know, but she was clever. She could have done something with that talent of hers.'

Harriet went over to the rocking horse and climbed on its back, as she'd often done when we were children. It creaked as she rode to and fro. Mounted on the spotted palfrey with its flaming nostrils and grey mane, she looked like a middle-aged page riding through a tapestry forest.

'Sir never gave your poor mother a chance to draw or paint — or even have a cup of coffee, for that matter. He wanted her around the whole time. 'Bunny, come here.' 'Bunny, where are you?' 'Where's Bunny? Tell her I want her.' She never had a moment. Only sometimes when he was filming she managed a sketch or two. You know those drawings I showed you? The ones she did in Hollywood.'

I had wanted one of them. Harriet had not offered it to me.

'She was a dear girl. A dear girl. The best pair of legs in the ballet,' Harriet said, climbing off the horse.

As she was leaving the studio she said:

'By the by, Tam's not bad. I saw her at the rehearsal. She was making them laugh.'

'Thank the Lord.'

'*You* pulled the fat out of the fire, didn't you?'

It was Harriet's sort of compliment: I was never sure if it was a dig.

'I didn't do it by myself. The doctor wasn't there but a friend of his was and he drove me to find them. They were in a beat-up old house in Camden Town.'

'Johnnie and Tam? How did they get there?'

'Ask Johnnie. It was falling to bits. Full of drunks.'

'Charming,' said Harriet as if she didn't mind in the least. 'Johnnie and Tam have an odd way of enjoying themselves. The crummier the party the more they fancy it.

51

Maybe it's Tam's reaction from Sir and putting on the style. Like a boy whose mother's always scrubbing at his face when he's a kid, so he goes round with it dirty when he's twenty.'

She went out, shutting the door quietly. She was the only member of the family who didn't slam.

The sky clouded, and the dark green tops of the elms began to shake as a wind sprang up. Through the open windows came a smell like rain.

\* \* \*

I went back to studying my father's gloves. They creased as if Dad were gripping something. Dad gripped hard. I remembered another pair of hands I had noticed to-day. They were strong too, but not trained to express thoughts or to beckon you into subjection. Broad hands, rather pale, with fair hair on the back.

There was a knock on the door.

'Don't knock, Harriet. Come in!'

It was a surprise to see Mrs. Brown's pale face.

'I am so sorry to disturb you.'

'Disturb me any time,' I answered sharply. Mrs. Brown seemed stuck with that meek secretarial manner; she didn't need to use it on me.

'Sir Robert wants you.' Her head, bodiless, a head on a pike at the Tower, was all I could see round the door. Apparently the body wasn't coming into the room. By this she was indicating how hard-worked she was. Who questioned it?

'But he's rehearsing,' I said. I didn't get up but sat at the easel, staring at what I could see of her.

'He's returned from the theatre, and there's been a planning meeting. He says He wants you right away.'

It was quite an achievement the way Mrs. Brown managed to speak of Dad in capital letters. He wants. He says. He is.

'But did he say what he wants me *for*, Mrs. Brown?'

'I can't tell you, Miss Waring. He did not inform me.'

I longed to say, 'Call me Candida,' but it wouldn't do any good. She would consider it disrespectful to my father. And anyway she wasn't going to last. I doubted if the most ingenious in-fighting on my part would keep her the job for more than a few months longer. I knew the signs.

She waited until she saw I was safely on my feet, then disappeared rather suddenly.

I went thoughtfully downstairs.

Father didn't usually send for me twice in the same day. Had he heard anything about Tam? Surely it wasn't possible. Yet Father's intuition about both his daughters was uncanny, and was something we had had to take into account all our lives.

Suppose he *had* heard about Tam's escapade; did I march in and tell him a downright lie? I slowed my steps to a crawl trying to prepare myself for a number of different contingencies.

Father was signing letters at an outsize desk by the window. He always held his planning meetings in the drawing-room, because the study was too small. The meeting usually consisted of five or six people: the stage director, two casting directors, the company manager, literary and publicity managers. Apparently they had all just gone: coffee cups lay around, and bars of cigar smoke floated in the still air. Harriet, clearing away, caught my eye and winked.

She wasn't worried anyway.

My father had changed from the old jeans and sweater he wore at rehearsal into a particularly handsome blue silk suit. I loved to see him dressed up. His glossy hair shone; his throat rose like a column from a white shirt; he looked beautiful and extraordinary.

He also looked happy, and I considered saying:

'So Teddy's funny after all.'

But sometimes when we were flip he turned into ice, and I didn't want that just now.

He swivelled round.

'There you are, Candy.'

The nickname. He used it rarely. And when he did so, I always wished he wouldn't. It was as if he put a finger on a particularly weak part of my heart. Suppose my heart to be a pear. Father found the spot where it was going soft.

'The meeting went really well to-day. We're all set for our new London season,' he said. 'Like to hear what we're doing?'

It touched me that he had sent for me to tell me his plans. When he did things like that I was . . . almost . . . his slave.

'First, we're doing *Cherry Orchard*, concurrent with the Ghilain farce. *Orchard* opens in six weeks. That's good, isn't it?'

'And you'll play Gayev?'

'Right.'

'How lovely.' He had played the part before and made me cry.

He looked up quickly, unable to resist the sound of love and admiration. He looked at me just then with real love in return. We beamed at each other.

'Then we're reviving *Pericles*; I'm directing and I'm giving the lead to Maurice. Then a play by a new Swiss author. Very odd. We're quite excited about it. Finally, with luck, we'll get Jack Harris's new play — he promised it to us by then. It seems to be working out a stunner. With a funny part for me. So we'll have Ghilain, Chekhov, Shakespeare and two mods.'

I said it sounded wonderful.

He looked at me with a friendly face and chuckled.

There was no frown and no sign of trouble. I had been stupid to bother that he might have heard about Tam. I was glad he wanted to talk to me, and I sat looking at the top of his head as he bent to finish signing the pile of letters.

He said, in the throwaway voice he used for comedy:

'We start rehearsing *Orchard* immediately the Ghilain has opened. Going to be tough, doing something as difficult as the Ghilain and rehearsing another play just as difficult at the same time.'

'You've all done it before.'

'True, true. Actors like to be worked to death.'

'What about your Athens film?'

'Silas rang. Says he'll wait,' Father said simply. I thought: '*Of course he'll wait. And so will everyone else in the world if they're going to get you.*'

Then my father said casually.

'By the by. Just one small thing. We've been doing the casting for *Orchard* this afternoon, and I've cast you as Anya. Nice part. You start rehearsing in ten days' time.'

# 3

When you're frightened of something and have been subconsciously waiting for it, there's a moment of fearful relief when it happens.

It was like that now.

I spoke carefully.

'But Dad. You know I can't act any more.'

My father gave an impatient sudden movement as if brushing away a fly.

'I mean it, Dad.'

'Tut. Don't be childish, Candida. You're a big girl now!'

He made the silly phrase sound funny, dropping his jaw and giving me a comedian's sly look.

I couldn't help smiling.

'Big enough to know what I can do, and what floors me,' I said.

He brushed the fly away again, surprised that it had come buzzing back. But his eyes were ominous. I had never been afraid of my father or — except on stage — under his extraordinary spell. In New York, my failure had been my own. It had hurt because I revered him. A frozen amateur cluttering up

the stage had no place beside such beauty and such power.

Free of the magic and menace he used on other people, I was now only scared that we would hurt each other as father and daughter.

'Darling,' I said, 'you really will have to give up your idea of making me an actress. I know you always wanted it and I used to as well. But it is hopeless. A person can't help having no talent. I thought you'd accepted it. After all, you do have Tam. Why can't she play in *The Cherry Orchard*?'

'She's far too young and silly to tackle Chekhov yet. As you know perfectly well,' he said, his tone as friendly as mine. He managed to indicate that we'd talked over her future often before, conspiring together for Tam's success.

'Yes, yes, we've got Tam on the road,' he said. 'Now we must return to the problem of Candida.'

He picked up a paper-knife and laid it on the flat of his hand. The Moscow Art Theatre had given it to him; it was silver, the handle shaped like an ear of corn. Russian words, mysterious as a rune, were lettered along the blade.

'*The Orchard*'s a beautiful play. His best. You always told me it was a favourite of yours,' he said, looking at the ceiling.

'It is.'

'Then why — '

'Oh Dad!' I was growing exasperated. 'Please don't let's go round in circles. Do accept it. I can't act again, I really can't!'

I leaned forward to take his hand. But it held the knife. I went on, talking faster.

'We both found out in New York that I was no good and wasn't ever going to be. You *must* have got used to it by now. Everything's settled down, hasn't it? You don't have to worry about me, I'm happy and I've started to paint. I'm doing well at art school. I've made good progress, the principal's pleased with me . . .'

He interrupted my anxious speech with a loud snort of derision. Throwing down the knife, he swivelled round in his chair, the arms of which were two mahogany claws. He put a hand on either claw, a Roman consul in judgment. He was always reminding me of characters I'd seen him play on the stage.

'Candida, listen. You can start by forgetting that balderdash about art. There's only one art for a Waring and that is the drama. I've made up my mind, you are going to play Anya. The character suits you. It's delicate. Youthful. Very instinctive. I admit you'll find it difficult. The part is demanding, the play very subtle. It's been done wonderfully by the

Russians; that sets a precedent. They'll expect us to be good. And coming back won't be easy for you. Why should it be? *I* found it difficult in My early years. You'll have to face gruelling work.'

'Work!' I cried, my voice rising, my good resolves vanishing. 'Do you think I care about hard work! What I care about is not being able to act! I hated being no good — I loathed it! You don't know what it was like, playing with you and knowing every night I was getting worse. You shan't make an actress of me! It's cruel of you!'

'You'll do as I say!' His voice was louder, so much stronger than mine.

'I tell you, I can't.'

'Rubbish, woman, you will TRY!' he shouted, and he sprang to his feet and seized both my hands, pulling me up with him. He gripped my hands so tightly that I winced. He stared at me with his brilliant eyes and he said softly:

'And you will have ME.'

With an effort as hard as dragging myself out of a huge current in the sea, I pulled away my hands.

'I won't go through it all again, I won't, I won't,' I sobbed, running from the room.

⋆　⋆　⋆

61

It was dusty late afternoon as the bus lumbered through the streets near Shaftesbury Avenue. My thoughts turned drearily over and over, getting nowhere. How could my father try for a second time to make a silk purse out of a sow's ear? That's what I was: the sow's ear. I'd lived all my life with actors and had believed myself one of them. It had hurt to find out that I wasn't, and hurt worse to say so to my father. The true actor was an instrument of the writer, poet and filmmaker, adding magical and subtle ingredients to their work, reflecting humanity and telling it something more about itself. I had hoped to be all that. To be an actor, you needed to be a selfless egotist: as my father was. He sacrificed time, sleep, holidays, comfort, money, health, for his art. Yet it was for Waring, always for Waring: for Waring's long, long love affair with the public.

It did love him, that great treacherous animal that makes an audience. And the love had always been two-way. My father needed them as much as they needed him, needed to know they loved *him*, wanted *him*, were in tune with *him*. He bathed in that love and it nourished him. He wanted to make me be its extension, as he had made Tam. The Waring girls must show they could tame the animal too.

Through our childhood, my father had been a perfect parent. He had given us a double love because we had no mother. He was firm, fierce, tender. It was wonderful how he could make us laugh. Whoever wanted his time, directors and financiers, managements and actors, playwrights and journalists, musicians and designers, he kept a thick slice for Tam and me. He was our father, he studied and understood us.

Why didn't he know how much he hurt me now? There wasn't a girl with talent who wouldn't jump at the chance to follow a distinguished father into such a career, as the sons and daughters of other famous actors had done. Who'd choose instead to be upstairs sketching a pair of gloves?

Miserable, in some way guilty, I felt I must talk to my sister. She was practical and impulsive and I needed her. It was a sour sort of joke that only a few hours ago I'd been worrying about my father and Tam, and now I myself was running to Tam for help about him.

I got down from the bus and walked the rest of the way to the theatre, crossing a square where lanky sycamores grew, their roots cracking the pavement. I went down an alleyway of old shops, past a jeweller's in whose windows were dusty gold half-hunters, and the engagement rings of dead Victorian beauties.

My father's theatre company was only recently founded. Until then he'd been the freelance star actor making his rich living by being invited by any one of London's impresarios to appear in a single play put on for a run. But his taste, always with the present though never in advance, had recently changed. He now ran his own State-aided permanent ensemble, and used the fashionable system of staging a number of productions in repertory, giving the public a varied programme of plays to choose from. He'd fought against his own desire to alter the acting habits of his life. He was an actor first and an actor last and the complications of repertory might prevent his talent burning so consistently, might limit the limitless feat of enslavement.

But Dad always matched the times. He'd set up his own company, working a repertory system of classic and modern plays, and had collected together clever young men of the theatre who, as well as coping with the main work, had also started a school to train actors and experiment with new techniques.

Very odd some of the experiments were, but Dad, delighted with the novelty, went into them heart and soul. He discovered that readings, mime, acrobatics, were all grist to his mill. He plunged into a new and varied world, and became its heart — 'We can still show them,' he had said to me, winking.

The theatre that was now his was the old Royalty, a playhouse which had been staggering along when Dad arrived with his company, his gleaming eyes, his subsidy and his art. The empty box office started to see queues. The place, like Dad, changed overnight.

The Royalty, built in 1905, was florid. A sculpted frieze of dour-faced muses decorated the façade, like Edwardian girls trooping off to tennis. Dad liked those muses. He said the tragic one with the bob was Harriet. The place, dilapidated when Dad arrived in his Rolls, now glittered. Carpet the colour of peonies bloomed in the foyer, brilliant posters shone on the front of the house. When you went into the theatre, it hummed with life like a successful factory.

I went down to the stage-door to find out if my sister was rehearsing. Some of the directors, mostly those of my father's generation, disliked visitors at their rehearsals. My father, reared on this mystery and secrecy, was quick to notice that it was out of date, and now in the new openness and freedom any one among us was welcome at rehearsals. We went in quietly, sat as long as we liked and then slipped away.

The stage-door keeper had worked at the Royalty for twenty years. The past literally hung around Sidney. The walls of his cubby-hole were pinned with yellow photographs of dead actors and he never looked at them and never added any more. He had transferred his interest to horses. Sitting with Alice Delysia and Jack Buchanan tentatively smiling behind him, he studied form.

'Hallo, Sidney, okay if I go through?'

'Help yourself, Miss Waring.'

'My sister rehearsing?'

'That's right,' said Sidney, marking his evening paper with a pencil and wearing an expression that could only come from losing a week's pay.

I went down a stone passage and through the swing doors into the rehearsal room. It was as lofty as a church and had been a boxers' gymnasium. Ropes, leather horses, coconut mats and parallel bars remained. It was now used for rehearsals, fencing, mime and gymnastics. My father believed in strong physical training, tough as that for the ballet and the circus. At forty-eight he could jump higher and fence better than actors in their twenties. He was proud of his physical success and competitive about it. I found this touching. Not to-day. Nothing about Dad was touching to-day.

Twenty actors were scattered round the room, talking, drinking coffee or lying on the ground with their arms behind their heads. They waved and gave me melting self-absorbed smiles. At the far end of the hall a woman beckoned to me. It was Periandra Pratt.

She was sitting on the top step that led to the stage, surrounded as usual by men. Periandra, who was fifty, played goddesses, queens and whores, and was all three. She had huge short-sighted eyes, a nose like an eagle's beak and a neck like a stem on which her ugly fascinating face flowered. She was wearing a ground-length full skirt that actresses use when rehearsing for costume, so that their movements set whilst they are wearing something of the correct weight and swing.

'Candida, my child.'

She knew that she made me nervous, and gave a commanding smile.

'Are you looking for Tamara, by any chance? You seem very distrraite,' she said, rolling the French 'r.' 'Or does Sir need the support of his big daughter?'

She looked round at the four men, who laughed obediently. They laughed whenever

Periandra opened her mouth. Actors had given her a loving, unsuitable nickname: they called her 'Peachey.' Men adored her. Women felt otherwise.

'I thought I might have a coffee with Tam,' I muttered. I looked round to see if my sister had climbed up on the gymnasium horse. Being short, she liked looking over people's heads.

'So you might, so you might, except that she's just disappeared in *deep* conversation with that fetching Johnnie Buckingham,' said Periandra, who liked all boys under twenty-five. 'He's attractive, isn't he? But strange. Sir, I gather, doesn't like him.'

Her huge eyes looked at me, waiting for a reaction. A queen impatiently waiting for news from some meek maid-in-waiting whose face, later, she'd probably slap. Authoritative, greatly talented, invaluable to my father, who had played with her scores of times, she was passionately loyal to the Royalty company, and the worst gossip in the place.

'All the boys fancy Tam,' she observed. 'It's disgusting how sex sizzles in the dressing-rooms. Those fat legs of hers must be sexy. But I think you're much prettier, darling. You look so like my gorgeous Bobbie. Boys! doesn't she look like Sir?'

The actors chorused slavishly that I was the image of my father. I laughed. For a moment, in the theatre's atmosphere, enclosed, dangerously warm, I was at home. In one corner, a solitary actor was declaiming to himself:

' 'I remember at the Embassy when the Prince Esterhazy complimented me personally . . . ' Damn! What comes next?'

He consulted his script.

Another actor had climbed the parallel bars and was hanging upside down, comfortable as a bat.

Periandra studied me, her mouth folded, her lips cracked where the lipstick had worn off. She dabbed absently at her hair, dyed a greyish mink, and shoved in a hairpin.

'We all know your big news, darling, so don't bother being mysterious. You're our new Anya. And *I* am playing Charlotta Ivanovna, your governess, remember, so I intend to keep you in order. Come along now, attention please. Hup!'

She smacked her hands sharply together.

The boys laughed and turned their friendly eyes on me again, regarding me as a new member of the company. The warmth went: I felt freezing cold.

Periandra slightly raised her voice to re-command the male attention.

'Five weeks' rehearsal time but *I* can do it

in two. I've played Charlotta three times before and my German accent is superb.'

No one answered. It was never necessary with Periandra. Her back as erect as a member of the Royal family, skirts billowing, eyes shining, she continued:

'Did I tell you about the Command Performance we gave one night at Windsor, when the Duke said . . . '

Her thrilling voice followed me as I walked away. The words sounded just as artificial as those about Prince Esterhazy . . .

★ ★ ★

It was late and the shadows stretched across the lawn in attenuated shapes when I went into the garden. Sheba, the family retriever, a glossy black bitch four years old, rushed towards me, waving a palm of a tail.

'Sheba, Sheba,' I said, kissing the head as shiny as a seal's.

I sat down on a grassy bank and the dog sat beside me, leaning her solid weight against me.

Harriet came out of the house, shading her eyes in the sunset, and when she saw me she came slowly over and sat down on the grass beside me. With Sheba on one side and Harriet on the other I felt guarded.

70

'I suppose you know the news. Everybody does.'

'Yes, Anya,' said Harriet. 'Sir came down to the kitchen to tell me. Delighted with himself.'

'Oh God.'

'He's out to dinner, by the way.'

'Disappearing after throwing a thunder-bolt.'

'Usual tactics. He said if you asked, he was seeing a Swedish impresario that you knew. Lars. The butch one.'

Sheba put her big head on my lap and I stroked it and sighed in a groaning kind of way so that Harriet gave a snort.

'Who can fight Dad?' I asked.

'You can.'

'Don't be stupid.'

'You *look* like Sir, but you take after your mother. She only stood up to him when she was in the right. Are you right?'

'Of course I am! I *can't* start acting again, Harriet. I just can't. I'd be even worse than in New York. I'd let him down and myself too. It would be a nightmare. I'd rather die.'

'Tell him in the morning, then,' she said, standing up. And she quoted my words to her in the kitchen this morning, 'He can't eat you.'

'Oh yes he can,' I quoted drearily back.

71

★ ★ ★

It was after nine o'clock when Tam's taxi drew up and she jumped out, let herself into the house and slammed the front door loudly behind her. I hurried down the stairs to meet her just as Harriet also appeared.

'The Polish Embassy rang,' announced Harriet with relish. She enjoyed bad news. 'A couple of officials want to come round to-night to talk about your father's award. Wouldn't do it on the telephone. Insisted on calling personally. Mrs. B. was supposed to cope but she has gone home with a headache, you'll be amazed to hear. I said I'd ring the Embassy back.'

'We'll see them,' Tam said promptly. 'And we'd better change our clothes,' she added, looking pointedly at me.

'Dinner will be five minutes and the Poles said they could come about nine-thirty, so you'd better look slippy,' said Harriet.

'Can't we eat in the kitchen?' I asked. Not for the first time.

'Sir doesn't like it. Up and change, please,' snapped Harriet, sounding like Periandra sounding like Charlotta.

My sister ran up the stairs ahead of me, singing. No one would have imagined she had been up all night and since then had worked for ten hours.

'That award Dad's got is the best one the Polish give for the arts, you know,' she said. 'I've checked. And the Hungarians are giving him one too at their festival.'

Tam loved Dad's fame. Foreign awards. Title. She talked a lot about them, kept a scrap-book of Dad's doings, meetings with Royalty, first nights, notices, articles, photographs, programmes.

'Someone has to be his Boswell,' she said, when people admired the book, now running into its third volume. 'I plan to figure rather largely in it myself later on.'

When we came downstairs again, Tam was in yellow silk, which suited her hair the colour of marigolds, and I was wearing a black and cream linen dress my father had brought me back from Finland.

'We look like Sir's daughters,' said Tam. She was always one for that.

Dinner was laid in the dining-room, loomed over by expensive badly-painted portraits of my father. Harriet made jokes about the one of Dad at twenty-five in *As You Like It* — 'He always sits at the table with Orlando just behind him. To give someone the chance to say you haven't changed a bit.'

'Well, he hasn't!' cried Tam. Harriet and I

exchanged glances. Now and again Tam's loyalty was tedious and suspect.

'I suppose I'm wasting my time to suggest you press the bell by your foot when you're ready,' Harriet said, serving the soup.

'I'm not ringing for you,' I answered as usual.

'*I* don't mind ringing if it save time and helps Harriet,' put in Tam in an apple-pie-and-cream voice.

'No one is ringing for anyone,' I said. 'Tam can pop to the kitchen and get the next course.'

When Harriet had gone out of the room I said:

'I've told you and told you. One doesn't press a bell to summon a friend.'

'She always asks us to.'

'What's that got to do with it? How are you going to make an actress if you don't know what people feel?'

My sister shrugged. She was not to be put out this evening. She ate her soup saying it was delicious and she was sure it was solid potatoes.

'I'm starting my diet to-morrow, first thing. I saw myself sideways in the glass in the Green Room. I bulge as if I was pregnant. The new diet's one the models use in Paris. I cut it out of *Elle*. Steak and

74

champagne and that's all.'

'Father won't let you drink.'

'He can't disapprove when he sees I lose six pounds in three days,' she exclaimed plaintively. 'The steak's for protein and the champagne's for lift and sugar, they said in the article. I like the sound of that. Lift and sugar. I get quite *funny* on champagne. Might improve my playing. Harriet's promised to get in loads of steak just as if I were a boxer and pile it into the frig ready to keep my strength up for Midinette. She — in case you don't know — is the one I'm playing in the Ghilain. I have told you about the part, darling, but you don't hear a thing I say.'

'You're very spirited to-night. I suppose Midinette is going well.'

'She's been a bit slippery till now but I think I'm getting her at last. Do you remember that ancient school-mistress, Miss Antony, who used to say we girls mustn't be 'pert'? Midinette's pert. Impertinent and after a tip. Pleased with herself. Not respectful to her betters. I wouldn't have her making my hats.'

My sister's face was absent. For the time being the character had become herself, yet separate from herself. She walked in and out of it, possessing another body and another soul.

When actors speak of the roles they are playing, they speak in the third person: not 'When I play Hamlet I shall be . . . ' but 'Hamlet is bitter because . . . ' 'Polonius isn't a fool, he's cunning and he thinks . . . ' With some, the characters they take on never fall to the ground like discarded clothes when they leave them. Each character continues to live a mysterious life of its own, to have a past and sometimes a future. If you ask an actor who has played the role what Hamlet felt as a child at the Danish court, he can tell you.

'Midinette's much too fond of money. Always working out how much everything costs. You'd be surprised the cash she digs out of people for knowing other people's secrets. She's in the nosy-parker business.'

'What sort of hats does she make?'

'Fantastic. Real creations,' said Tam, who'd never herself sewn on a button that didn't come off.

'It sounds rather good.'

'Yes and no. It's the middle of the play that's difficult.'

I did not answer. I had read the play and the middle was funny. What Tam meant was, 'My role isn't working in the middle.' 'Midinette falls in love with the butler and then her character simply collapses and she's soppy till the final curtain. I don't believe that a person completely alters when they fall in love. I mean, of course they go off their heads. And they're hellish boring to be with. Aren't they boring? But they don't change. A person's nature seems to me to set very early in life. It's like concrete. For a short time, all sloppy in the mixer. And then suddenly there it is. Rock!'

'Neither of us is particularly expert in what happens when you fall in love,' I felt bound to say.

'You have been a couple of times,' said Tam, always interested in the way I was feeling and inclined to question me so closely that I recognised the actor at her studies.

'A bit. Never head over heels.'

'I was head over heels once,' said Tam with pride.

She was referring to the time when she was fifteen and had a crush on one of my father's actors, a handsome, eccentric man who'd played Mercutio. He'd been fond of Tam rather as if it were Sheba galloping at his heels.

'The diet's to-morrow so it doesn't matter what I eat to-night,' Tam said helping herself to more mashed potato. 'Harriet's put nutmeg on these.'

'You saw Johnnie again to-day.' It seemed a pity to break her benevolent mood.

'Periandra!' exclaimed Tam indignantly. 'Silly old witch, she told me you'd been at rehearsal. Why doesn't she take her beady eye off me?'

'Why must it be Johnnie? You're not falling for him now, are you?'

My sister looked at me cautiously, her hair falling on her cheeks as if she were looking through a curtain. I'd seen the same look on my father's face, it reminded me of an animal at the mouth of its burrow. It was a paradox that this cautious peering creature could be subsequently found on stage — extravert — dead centre — bathed in the glare of lights.

'You know Dad can't bear him,' I said.

'Are you saying I must toe the line with Dad all the time, fall in with his whims, have my friends screened by him, perhaps? You're not on very strong grounds, mate. *I* haven't got Dad on my conscience. *I'm* working for him. *I'm* acting my head off.'

'So you are.'

'Oh, cheap, cheap,' she jeered.

'You still haven't said what's the attraction of Johnnie Buckingham.'

'Aunty,' she said witheringly. 'It's your worst part. You ham it. I like Johnnie B. because he makes me laugh and he's a nice boy and original and he needs me. He has a horrible time and I'm going to help him.'

Tam loved a good cause.

'Perhaps you should concentrate on helping yourself by playing Midinette really well.'

Tam's plump face went pink. Even her nose reddened.

'I should think you ought to be bothering about how you're going to play Anya. That'll shut you up.'

Silence.

'You've heard.'

'Of course I've heard,' she said impatiently. 'The whole of the Royalty has heard, including Sid. And if Periandra wasn't afraid of Sir, she'd have told her pal on the *Sunday News*, who pays her linage, if you ask me, for those mysterious little leaks about the company which are always getting into that paper. Periandra saw the *Orchard* cast-list Dad was holding, while he was giving us notes after the rehearsal. She read it upside down. She had a lover once who was a printer and he taught her to read upside down. She said it's proved very useful.'

I was too dispirited to smile.

'I can't act again.'

'Ridiculous!'

'I can't. I've told him I can't. He simply won't accept it.'

'Of course he won't,' she said, cutting

79

herself a thick slab of melon. She was quite unsympathetic. Sometimes she was warm and sometimes cold, it was no good relying on the weather with Tam.

'I do wish you'd stop looking so doleful,' she exclaimed, after a moment. 'That face of yours is very annoying.'

I couldn't help laughing. 'Why?'

'It's maddeningly like Dad's. I've always envied you the Waring face, haven't I? Still, I have got his eyes. That's one blessing. You'll have to get used to acting, darling, and be an old pro like me. Lots of actors lose their nerve the first time.'

Harriet came in with some raspberries and I said:

'There isn't going to be a next time. I can't do it and that's that. Don't you agree, Harriet?'

'Squabble it out between you.. I'm busy,' muttered Harriet and left the room.

'I came to the theatre this afternoon to ask you to help me,' I said, wishing Harriet had stayed to give me support.

'The boot's suddenly on the other foot, isn't it?' said Tam, warm again. She loved being asked for help.

'Tam. There's something you really could do. Better, much better, than I can. Talk to Dad for me.'

She stared at me.

'You can explain how I feel. And you'll do it coolly. I know I shall get upset and start yelling. You're clever with him when you want to be. And very persuasive.'

She said slowly: 'I wish I could.'

'Of course you can. Please, darling! I'm sure he'd listen to you.'

'Did he listen to you?' she exclaimed. 'And do you think I have the slightest influence over him about the theatre now I work for him? The whole thing between Dad and me is different now when it's to do with acting . . . And what isn't to do with acting? He's just as loving, just as awful, but it's different, because he knows what I'm thinking and what my motives are all the time. How can I stick up for you when he knows I'd give my eye teeth for Anya? He'd merely use how I feel to prove that *you* must feel the same. He'd make me look a fool. When Dad talks to me as one actor to another . . . he's *got* me.'

It was true.

'Perhaps he'll get you too . . . ' said Tam.

★ ★ ★

We had scarcely finished supper when the front door bell rang; there were voices in the hall, and Harriet came in to say: 'The Polish

81

lot are here. I've put them in the drawing-room. I'll serve coffee right away.'

'What are they like, Harriet?' asked Tam, springing up. 'Is one of them handsome?'

'As an angel!' said Harriet, putting a hand on her breast and staggering.

My sister and I went into the drawing-room together. Two men were standing unanchored in the centre of the room. They were dressed in dark badly-fitting clothes and had clumsy brown shoes. One man was youngish, white-faced, and sharp-nosed; the other, a burly peasant with a bullet head and the shoulders of an ox. He was holding a plastic attaché-case.

We shook hands and I asked them to sit down.

Tam and I sat, our backs as straight as Periandra's, facing our diplomatic visitors.

I spoke in French (Tam knew almost none) while Harriet brought in the coffee, which she placed carefully in front of me: silver pot, Sèvres cups, engraved tray. It looked like something out of the People's Museum in Warsaw. I thought it very unsuitable.

While the men were replying to my banal remarks with phrases as banal, they looked curiously round the room. It was full of photographs of celebrities, paintings, tro-phies, the variety of objects that famous

82

people are given by those who love or admire them . . . the Russian vase with a dragon on it, the Indian bell, the shiny Oscar on the piano. A painting of Dad as Malvolio grimaced over the fireplace. Below was a rapier given to Dad by the King of Denmark.

The visitors drank their coffee and continued to talk. Their voices were soft and full of sounds as if they were hushing a child. I looked at them and they gazed back. We couldn't communicate. Even their smell was different, of cigarettes and soap and sweat differently constituted from ours. The distance of carpet between us was vast: seas and mountains and deserts and cornfields lay in it.

The bullet-headed man, with a gleam of steel teeth, explained that they wished to know if Sir Robert Waring could come to the Ambassador's reception next Thursday, as His Excellency was to present him with the Order of the Red Star of Art, First Class.

'It is very magnificent. My father will be honoured to attend,' I said. 'The whole family is greatly honoured, are we not, Tamara?' I added in English.

'So. So. Your sister has a Russian name.'

Both men smiled at her.

Tam gave them, in return, the smile she had christened her slow burn.

To be a famous actor is to have a passport into every country in the world and we were used to vicarious diplomatic admiration. We nodded like those old china mandarins whose heads nod slowly for minutes when you merely touch them with a finger. We offered them slices of goodwill as if it were cake.

'There is one thing,' said the big man who did the talking. 'We have been instructed to bring something else to Sir Robert Waring. It comes from the Polish people to a great artist. You will understand why we asked special permission to come to-night. We could not wait for the Embassy occasion. And as Sir Robert Waring is not here, we present it to his daughter.'

He picked up the attaché-case, placed it on his knee, and snapped it open. He took out what looked like a large cigar box.

'This has been named after your father. It is the first perfect specimen of its strain in our country.'

He put his hand into some cotton wool.

In his hoarse hushing voice he announced: 'The Waring.'

Scarcely in full flower, thick petals heavily veined, it was a large, perfect rose.

The flower was a dark gleaming red, each petal seemed to be made of stiffened velvet. In places, the heart of the rose was almost black. It had a thick stalk and three dark green leaves.

We all stood up. Taking a step forward, he placed the flower in my hand. I stood quite still, holding it.

The rose, smelling sharply, named absurdly, flowered in my hand. It had been brought across a great distance. It had been named with love. Like great acting, it was beautiful and lasted a short time.

'My father will be proud . . . he will want to thank you very specially . . . '

Suddenly the man leaned forward and put heavy hands on my shoulders.

'He already has,' he said, and kissed me on both cheeks.

He gave me a smile. Every steel tooth shone.

Tamara and I waved as the black diplomatic car drove away. We went back into the drawing-room. The Waring lay on top of the piano.

Tam picked it up and smelled it. We looked at it in silence.

'How can you say you don't want to act,' she said at last, 'when it can make people do things like that?'

# 4

Early next morning I was wakened by voices in the drive. My father's voice, Tam's laugh, Mrs. Brown's respectful mutters. I lay and listened to my father sending both women scurrying on half a dozen errands before he finally drove away.

Silence washed back. And with it my uncomfortable thoughts. My resolve had been firm yesterday: I had been sure of it and of myself. I would not be drawn back into the theatre, I'd stand up to Dad because I knew I was right. I couldn't act, and he was cruel and vain to try to make me. Now I began to wonder. Tam had said that actors always lost their nerve at first. Was my father, versed in the theatre because he was the thing itself, right after all? Uneasy and miserable, I went downstairs to look for Harriet and coffee. In the hall was a large buff envelope addressed to me in my father's bold illegible writing.

I knew what it was before I tore open the envelope. A copy of *The Cherry Orchard*, with a sheet of paper which merely said 'Dad.' I wasn't surprised but I was furiously angry. I opened a drawer in the chest of drawers where we kept Sheba's lead and shoved the play out of sight.

I was working in the studio when Harriet came up to say I was wanted on the telephone.

'It isn't Sir, so don't start like that. Ventura took the message and she did tell me it wasn't him. But she pronounces names so appallingly that most of the country's famous actors sound like Italian boy-friends. I don't know who else it could be. Johnnie asking you to smoke reefers in Camden Town?'

She looked pleased at her mild joke. She had a soft spot for Johnnie and probably encouraged Tam.

'Candida?' said a man's voice, when I answered the telephone. 'Ben Nash. I've got some good news. Your friend Johnnie went home on the sleeper to Newcastle last night. As a matter of fact I saw him off. He'll be out of London for a couple of weeks at least, so you can stop worrying about your kid sister.'

'Oh,' I said. I swallowed a selfish remark about not worrying.

'Did you think I knee-jumped him into going on the train?' inquired Ben breezily. 'I didn't, you know. So rest your soft heart.'

I let him think it was soft.

'He's going up north because of his art exhibition. He has fifteen canvases so far and there's a new Northumberland school of student painters he's got an eye on. He's going to get some of their work together and bring it to London to startle us all. Incidentally, he's also left because your sister's busy rehearsing and hasn't any time for him just now.'

'Thank you very much for . . . '

'Not so fast. Aren't you going to give me the chance to ask you to lunch? What about to-day? We could go to Jack Straw's. What about in half an hour?' asked Ben Nash, whose technique was not to wait and see if I were going to hum and ha.

★ ★ ★

He was punctual, and I was glad to see him, but shy. He himself was in high spirits, talked all the way to Jack Straw's, and had booked a table with a view.

After we had ordered the meal I said:

'I've been thinking that I don't know anything about you except that you're a friend of Dr. Laurie's and have been staying with him.'

'Still am. My flat's being painted and the smell's unspeakable. Being a friend of your family doctor's makes me okay, doesn't it?'

'You're laughing at me.'

'No, I'm not. I think you're one of those girls with a soft spot for the Hippocratic Oath. All the nicest women have.'

'My father says my faith in doctors is idiotic. He says I only have to talk to one for five minutes and I get cured of everything from leg-ache to depression.'

'So pals of the doctors are okay,' repeated Ben, putting too much butter on his roll. 'And Chris Laurie loves me.'

'You still haven't told me what you are, what you do or anything. You know much too much about me.'

'Everybody knows about you,' he said, with his mouth full. 'Sir's daughter.'

'How do you know he's called that?'

'Everybody knows that too.' He still told me nothing about himself, and of course I was curious. We talked during the meal, and he showed the same lively curiosity about everything I said and did, made jokes at which he laughed himself, looking at me with bright grey eyes, as if he also found the world a joke and me a part of it. He had vitality; he was tough and somehow sexy. He was also protective; I felt looked-after. More than when I was with actors. Much more.

At the end of the meal I returned to the point that intrigued me.

'Ben.'

'I like the way you pronounce my name. You have a delicious voice.'

'You haven't yet told me what you do.'

'Haven't I?' he said.

'Do tell me. You know all about me: it is very one-sided.'

'Promise not to hold it against me.'

'Why should I hold it against you?'

'Because I'm a journalist.'

I felt chilled. It explained everything: the manner; the knowledge of my family; the over-developed interest. Dad had always disliked and discouraged newspapermen to an absurd degree and had once hit a quite distinguished journalist on the jaw because his 'profile' of Dad had offended him.

'Tell them nothing,' he always said. 'Let them make it up.'

'But Dad, that's dangerous.'

'It is more dangerous to be friends with them. I know what I'm talking about. They're fickle and malicious, and don't know good acting from cheap ham,' he had said simply.

'You're very quiet.' Ben Nash broke into my thoughts. 'You must be taking it badly.'

'I was thinking it explained everything.'

'Now don't be silly!' he said, and tried to take my hand but I pulled it away. He was not offended, and laughed.

'If you think I've been sucking up to you to

get some show-biz secrets, you're more naïve than you should be. Grow up, girl. What single question about your father's plans have I dragged from you? What have I asked that any man wouldn't ask a pretty woman he was lunching with? Of course I'm interested in you. Everybody is. You're one of a famous family. But I won't insinuate myself into your confidences and publish them. Believe me.'

'I don't know.'

'I see you've inherited Sir Robert's fear of the Press. Trust me. I'm a trustworthy character.'

This time I let him take my hand. When he clasped it, I had little shivers down my spine.

'Very well,' I said at last.

'Good. That's settled, then.'

He started to talk about his job, on a weekly magazine that dealt mainly with politics, education and the arts. He was a man who enjoyed telling rather elaborate anecdotes, and he began one about a grandson of the writer Ghilain, author of the farce now being rehearsed at the Royalty. I was only half listening. I kept wondering if I could trust Ben Nash as a friend. My father would have exploded if he'd known I was lunching with a member of the Press, let alone considering telling him my troubles. But I did trust Ben Nash and his masculine, easy, optimistic way.

When he'd finished his story and there was a pause I said:

'I'm worried about something.'

'I know.'

'What do you mean?'

'I saw you in the street last night. You were out walking by yourself. You looked miserable. That's why I rang.'

'Oh.'

'Come on, Candida,' he said, studying my face. 'Try me. Tell me the trouble.'

'My father wants me to go back to the theatre.' It didn't sound enormous.

Ben didn't react. 'I gathered from what you *haven't* said that you gave it up,' he said. 'Why did you?'

'It gave me up. I was no good.'

'I never heard that.'

'It was in New York. I wasn't very important. Just bad.'

'What did your father say when he told you he wanted you to act again?'

'That he'd cast me in a new production, a big part.'

'You said you couldn't do it?'

'Of course. He knew it anyway. I told him when I got back from America that I couldn't — that I didn't want to walk on to a stage ever again. I told him again a few months ago.

Then he coolly says I'm in his next production.'

'Why don't you just refuse?'

'You don't know Dad, only *about* him. You might as well argue with a north wind. If only someone would stick up for me. Support me. Everybody I know is connected with Dad, works for him, needs his good opinion. Who'd tell Dad to leave me alone? Except my doctor, I suppose.'

'Your doctor wouldn't give you a medical certificate to say you shouldn't act, unless it was going to make you ill,' he said, smiling slightly. 'Is it?'

'Of course not! I'm perfectly well. Just miserable. Who is right, Dad or me? I don't even know that I am. Yet the thought of trying to act again is like — like making a parachute jump. It really terrifies me.'

This time it was Ben who was thoughtfully silent, while I talked. I tried to be fair as I described our family, how the theatre was the food we ate, the air we breathed. I talked about my failure in New York, and about the art school. Finally, I described my meeting yesterday with my father.

Talking about that still upset me.

Ben said:

'No one can make you act, you know. No one can drag you on to the stage and say 'give a performance.' All your father can do is persuade you.'

'*All!*'

He smiled at my voice. 'How long does it take him to accept something when he finds he really can't change it?'

'That never happens.'

'Candida, don't be silly. You may all be larger than life, and have different values from other people, but your father isn't superhuman. Yesterday when we went off to Camden Town, you told me, and you believed it too, which made it so interesting, that nobody was ever late for him. That's patent rubbish. Suppose I was interviewing him and fell off a bus? Now you say that nothing he wants ever gets changed. He has a highly complicated life, there must be a lot of things that can go wrong. When they do he probably persuades everybody that he has for some reason manipulated things that way.'

That sounded like Dad, and in spite of myself I giggled.

'So. So,' Ben said, encouragingly, 'what happens when an actor he wants gets ill or a writer can't finish a play or that government subsidy he's always on about isn't big enough? Things go wrong. Then what happens?'

'But — '

'Yes, yes, the world revolves round him and he's its axis,' said Ben, firmly not mixing his metaphors. 'Just think. What happens?'

Silence.

'There was Ian Radcliffe, I suppose,' I said. 'He broke his Royalty contract to make a film and messed up the entire winter season after he'd been given a line of these lead parts. Then there was Jenny Dyson. My father dug her out of a rep in Cornwall and planned a play for her and she went off to Hollywood instead and did a bad musical.'

'Yeah. I remember Jenny Dyson. Clever girl but went to America too soon. What did your father do?'

'Was furious.'

'Of course. But what then?'

'He was just furious. He rampaged. It was awful. Boring and awful.'

'I don't have the impression that he frightens you, though,' Ben said coolly.

I was surprised. 'Of course he doesn't.'

'He frightens everyone else.'

'A lot of people. Or muddles them. He loves muddling them.'

'What happened *after* he rampaged?'

'I suppose he re-fixed things — and got over it,' I said, reluctant to admit it.

A pause. I stared at the table-cloth.

'And will get over you.'

95

'Don't you believe he will?' Ben asked. The restaurant was empty. The waiters had cleared all the tables but ours. It was high summer and mid-afternoon.

'Or does the idea of standing up to him frighten you after all?' Ben said, gently taking my hand again.

I was glad to hold his hand. 'No, he's never frightened me, though when he is really furious it *is* boring and exhausting, and he does put the fear of God into a lot of others and rather enjoys it, which is monstrous. It isn't that I'm particularly brave. I can just see the works all the time. What I feel about the acting thing is different. I feel I can't say no because of his work. Because he's a bit of a genius. How can one refuse a genius?'

'But if what he's asking you would hurt you and is beyond your power, you must. You must stand firm. Stand firm,' he repeated gently. 'Most of us are stronger than we know. Give yourself a chance to find out.'

Just for a moment, as we looked at each other, I was conscious of every physical thing about him. Of his grey eyes, fringed with fair lashes. Of his thick heavy blond hair, and his skin that looked as if it might go ruddy but never sunburn, and the fact that his ears stuck out. His mouth was wide, thin and curling. I wondered what it would be like to be kissed by him.

All we did was drive home and say good-bye.

★ ★ ★

I had been working in the studio all afternoon and was expecting my father to send for me. He was sure to do so, since we'd parted with nothing resolved last night and the copy of *The Cherry Orchard* was not going to be his last word. But there wasn't a soul in the house for hours. It was quiet and empty.

Suddenly the silence broke. One car after another began to drive up and to park in the drive, and when that was full the cars stopped nose-to-nose in the road outside. Bells and telephones rang. The noise of footsteps and voices rose up the well of the house. I went on to the landing and looked over the banisters to see crowds of people going through the open double doors of the drawing-room. Tam, wearing a dramatic white dress, saw me and signalled wildly.

I went back to get dressed. I took a long time, and chose something my father liked. He had the habit of noticing everything about Tam and me: the clothes we wore, our hair, fingernails, stockings and the pencil lines on our eyelids. He noticed too, nuances in our manner from day to day, particularly if these added or detracted from his particular requirements. He would demand that we altered our moods if they were not tuned to his, saying 'A bright face, please. Lift the face. The downward line puts ten years on the physiognomy,' or, quite as often, 'Don't snigger, girls, I want a serious discussion with sensible women and not a pack of tat on the Palace Pier.' He reminded me, not of a fond parent, but of a cook altering a dish to suit his taste by the addition of paprika, a spoonful of kirsch or some sweetening.

When I was dressed I went to the kitchen for news. I'd no intention of walking into the drawing-room without knowing what I was going to find.

The kitchen was simmering with work, the Italian lot polishing, exclaiming, and preparing food, Harriet snapping orders and rushing about.

She said promptly, 'Candida, pass the radishes out of the basket and keep them away from your dress. You look very nice dear and get out of my kitchen.'

'Harriet, *what* is going on?'

'The Compagnia della Robbia is going on. They are in London for a day or two on their way to the States for an American tour, and your father telephoned and asked them to stop off and see him. Sir wants to tie them up for a month in the winter while he's rehearsing the new Swiss play. When he gathered they could come he kept chuckling and rubbing his hands.' Harriet's thumbnail sketches of Dad made him more Shylock than Romeo.

'Your father asked us to get supper for twenty people, giving us lots of notice.' Harriet meant half an hour. 'Everybody in the kitchen, dear, hearing it's the della Robbia, is in a high old state. Ventura's spoilt the mayonnaise and had to start again three times.'

'Roberto is 'ere. Roberto 'imself,' said Ventura, red with exertion and emotion.

'She doesn't mean Sir. She means Vagnoli. Ventura is in love with him.'

'All Rome must love Roberto,' began Ventura, but Harriet shrieked, 'How many times have I said no garlic!'

She then pushed me out of the kitchen saying I was a bore and anyway Sir was waiting for me. At the door I remembered something.

'Harriet! I never told Dad about the rose named after him. How could I have forgotten!'

'Your sister never does. She told him.'

I waited.

'He rather liked it,' said Harriet, surprised.

★  ★  ★

The drawing-room was full of smiling, drinking, roaring people. They were all good-looking and noisy and their teeth flashed. I had noticed before that Italian actors *en masse* were absurdly handsome. No matter how many present-day hair styles and side-whiskers they had, they retained the haughty soft look of males in silent movies. The women were beautiful and reminded me of birds. Beaky. One particularly birdish woman, with a big nose and eyes that would have annoyed Periandra, had swooped on my father. A short man with a scarred face was flattering Tam. There was a smell of flowery scent and foreign cigarettes. Someone at the piano was playing startling sentimental music.

My father beckoned. I came up obediently to be introduced.

'Signora Graziella Terrosi, my child Candida.'

The bird woman gave me a huge meaningless smile and grasped my hand.

She looked at me and made a remark in Italian to Dad, who laughed and answered

100

with a great speech, also in Italian. I stood smiling resolutely. Dad was in high spirits. He loved talking Italian, which could well be one of the reasons he'd invited the della Robbia . . . apart from the fact that they always played to packed house, of course. Tam and the short actor joined us, and Dad, moving mercifully into English, told us all a bitchy story about a rival company. Everybody laughed. Dad and Graziella turned away, Tam was dragged off by one of the Royalty directors, and I was left with Tam's short friend. He was black-haired, with furrows down his cheeks as if rain had washed the flesh away. Dad always said that heavy lines could be an actor's fortune. This was Vagnoli, for whom Ventura had ruined the mayonnaise.

'Are you acting much now you do so much directing, Signor Vagnoli? I have seen all your films. We love them,' I said firmly. It was essential to place myself squarely with him if we were both to be comfortable.

'I do not act in pictures any more. One cannot direct them and be oneself in the middle, alas!' said Vagnoli. 'But in the theatre, yes. I play the husband in *El Scena della Matrimonio*.'

I was supposed to know the play and I hoped I looked as if I did.

101

'At present, I plan a film about Leonardo da Vinci. This will interest you,' said Vagnoli, who apparently thought me attractive, unless he gave these hot glances from habit. 'Lord Waring tells me you paint. I did not know in the family of the Lord was painting talent.'

Tam was standing very near me, and at this sentence she silently caught my eye, considering the new title.

'And the Lord also says you are to act in his new *Cherry Orchard*,' added Vagnoli.

Before I could reply my father (who had ears in the back of his head) spun round from his own conversation, putting an arm round my shoulders. He gripped me tightly as if to prevent me from falling. Grasped by my father's iron arm, I stayed still.

'Yes, she is to play Anya. My niece Anya. Would you say there's any resemblance?' My father bent towards me. He knew the effect of his face close to mine. The always-moving likeness of a parent and child in our case was very strong.

'Exquisite!' cried Graziella, clasping her hands.

'Very good!' echoed Vagnoli.

'She's to be a fresh little heartless Anya,' said Dad, cooing at me. 'Pretty and heartless,' he repeated. He looked down at me and sighed.

'Anya. No more. You are breaking my heart.' It was Gayev speaking.

The Italians applauded. Dad let go of me. I moved towards the piano out of reach.

Who would beat Dad on his own ground? He'd required me to look gooey, which I'd obeyed him by doing. I'd turned into the dear little real-life daughter or the dear little stage niece. Both. My resolve to escape from my father hardened now that I saw how busy he was, fixing it that I was caught. Tam without knowing it had described the way I now felt. My thoughts had been like cement 'all sloppy in the mixer.' Now they were turned to stone.

Dad had domestic laws as rigid as his theatre ones, and ever since we were children we were required to see guests off, not from the hall or the door but from the steps outside. We called this habit 'grouping.' Dad would call us to him, take his place dead centre, grasp a child by either shoulder, and all three of us would gracefully wave good-bye. Seeing off friends was a Waring production.

To-night we took our places, grouped, waved, until the last Italian compliment floated from the last car.

We came indoors. The house was mercifully quiet.

Dad gave a growling yawn.

103

'Luck, eh? The della Robbia for a month just when we need them with two comedies and a Pirandello. Good, ain't it?'

'Roberto and Graziella are brilliant,' said Tam piously. As usual, she'd been doing her homework. This time she did not get approval from Dad, who merely said 'Mm.'

We turned to kiss him good night, simultaneously bending forward. Dad accepted Tamara's kiss, pushing his cheek towards her and away from me.

'Good night, miss. Sleep tight and let's see if you can improve that entrance, to-morrow. You think about it and see if you can puzzle out what's wrong.' He pinched her cheek, looking at her indulgently. Then:

'I want to talk to you, Candida.' Without waiting for me he went off, humming, towards the drawing-room. Tam leaned over the banisters, made a face at me and crossed her fingers. I followed my father into the drawing-room and closed the door. He was pouring himself a drink.

'Will you have one?'

'No, thanks, Dad.'

'Good, good. I like to see you in training.'

I went across the room, drawn by the Polish rose sturdily flowering on the mantelpiece. It was as beautiful as yesterday, but a little bigger. My father lay back on the settee and closed his eyes. It was the moment to speak.

I couldn't say a word. I stared down at him. At the thick line where his dark hair, streaked with grey, sprang from his forehead. At the bump in the middle of his nose, that he sometimes claimed was from rugby and sometimes claimed was Greek. At the curling mouth with its sensual nether lip, and the throat, thick as the column of a temple. He opened his eyes and looked straight at me.

'My dear child. You are decided, aren't you?'

'Yes,' I whispered.

'And what is your answer?'

A pause.

'No, don't tell me. I can see it in your face,' he said.

'I'm sorry. I'm so sorry. Please, please believe me. You do know how I feel, dearest, don't you . . .'

I was braced for the storm as I spoke. But he was quite gentle. He continued to look at me from where he lay; his arms, lying along the top of the sofa, drooped.

And as I watched, my father seemed to diminish. He actually grew smaller. I had never seen till now that his hair was thinning, that there were deep bags under his eyes, that vitality was draining away and he was deathly tired.

'I would have liked to see you with me. To *have* you with me.' He rubbed his face over with his hand as if it were wet, dragging the pouches of flesh under his eyes.

'It's a bit sad,' he said at last.

'What is, darling?'

'Loving one's children.'

And then I simply could not bear it because there were tears in my father's eyes. He looked old and exhausted; he looked so horribly easy to hurt. With his pride, beauty and genius, it wasn't right that anyone should hurt him. I burst into tears and ran over, sobbing, to throw my arms round his neck.

'Oh, I'll do it! I'll try! But help me!' I think I said.

# 5

Tam and Harriet took the news that I was returning to the theatre with an annoying lack of surprise. My sister came into my room while I was still asleep the next morning. She was already dressed to go to rehearsal, and stood dramatically framed in the doorway, a habit she had caught from my father.

'Welcome back to the boards!'

Harriet already knew about me by the time I went down to the kitchen for breakfast, gave a brief smile and remarked that it was the first sensible thing I had done for months. She poured my coffee and left me. I was disappointed when I saw Harriet go. I always enjoyed her conversation with its stringent comment on my father or me or both of us. I'd hoped she would discuss my change of heart, whether she encouraged or teased.

Emotions often seemed to me to be like those masses of multicoloured wools that knitters thrust into knitting-bags or sewing-drawers. Some people can sort out the tangles and some can't. Harriet was one of those who can, she was patient, interested and never fooled. The knots, different colours and disorder never dismayed her.

Just as Tam's and Harriet's reactions disappointed me, so I found the following days tedious. Rehearsals for The Cherry Orchard were not starting yet, everyone at present was involved in the Ghilain farce. I had no challenge and excitement of starting work.

I tried to return to my drawing and painting, but when I went into the old nursery and sat down at the drawing-board I couldn't concentrate; every sketch seemed false. It was as if my wish to draw had been a spirit which deserted me the moment I said 'yes' to my father.

The weather was intensely hot, and I spent most of my time in the garden with the copy of The Cherry Orchard which I had to fish out of the drawer where I'd shoved it the other day. In the garden Sheba always joined me. She seemed to know I was worried, and sat stolidly beside me, leaning her weight against me as if protecting me from the invisible.

One thing did change. Whenever my father was at home, at early breakfast or between meetings, during snatched meals, late at night, he sent Mrs. Brown trotting round to find me. But when I joined him he never said a word about my playing again.

'Hallo, how's it going?' was all I got one evening. He put his head on one side.

'It's not *going* at all.'

Father appeared pleased.

'That's right, that's right, and just you wait until it does.'

He talked about his own work, about the way the farce was shaping — that the production had arrived at the moment when it needed an audience: without it the play was now a man with one leg. 'Yes, we must make 'em laugh. We must knock 'em off their seats.' He spoke like a clown in a circus. He often licked his chops over the thought of making people laugh, and had been heard to thunder at a poaching fellow actor, 'Hands off my gags!'

'Do you know something, Puss?' he said to me, one night when we were drinking hot milk in his study. 'An audience is much, much quicker in perception than the brightest single member of it. They get every nuance. They're so clever,' he said fondly.

He showed me his work, spread designs on the table in front of us, explained the miniature model sets, which stood like dolls' houses on his desk. He made me laugh a lot. He loved to mimic and sometimes mock the people he talked about, and his talent to evoke the person he mocked was uncanny.

109

Then he'd return again to work, and show me a photograph or a passage in a play, and talk about his productions or performances. Once, as I sat beside him, I thought that his manner to me was like that of a king in some last-century tale. Hadn't the kings spent great time and trouble to educate their children for a future of destiny? That was what Dad seemed to be doing: preparing me for a state marriage. He did not want me to miss a single nuance in my task, or an ounce of the weight of that crown he was going to drop on my head.

When I was with Dad, everything seemed possible. My father always had that effect, it was part of his Merlin character. He could woo gentle women of thirty to play fiends of fifty, and make middle-aged actresses succeed in the roles of girls. But when I was alone, avoiding thoughts of my fatal step back into my father's world, I preferred to think about Ben. I was attracted to Ben, and enjoyed his differences, all his differences, from the actors who had been my boy-friends.

In the past my father had watched actors taking me around with a sardonic interest.

'You're being run after, I see,' he would comment. And then, 'Maybe it's for your beautiful self, but somehow I think it's for a beautiful job.'

'Dad. How rude!'

My father looked pitying. 'When is an actor not an actor, my girl?'

He said exactly the same to Tam. He enjoyed reminding us that the Waring girls were surrounded by people wanting Him.

Ben Nash apparently did not want Dad, and Dad didn't even know I was interested in him. Was Ben interested in me? Perhaps not. It piqued me that I hadn't heard from him because his manner had been lively and promising, and once or twice I thought I'd made a conquest. Thinking about Ben, I wondered if it were a coincidence that both Tam and I preferred men who did not want a single thing from Dad.

★   ★   ★

With a splitting crack of thunder, summer vanished. Storms of rain knocked the petals off the syringa and scattered them, sodden and transparent, all over the lawn. Harriet was sour, Tam never home. One afternoon I took Sheba for a walk across the Heath. We were out for hours, wading through sodden grass or plodding down paths turned to rivers. We were alone. Everyone else had gone indoors to hide. It was nearly six in the evening when we slopped home, wet through.

At the corner by the bottom of the hill, locking his car, was Ben Nash.

His back was turned towards me, and I felt a lift of pleasure when I saw the fair-haired, heavy-shouldered figure in a pale raincoat.

'Hallo!'

He turned quickly, and when he saw me, gave exactly the smile I remembered.

'Hi. How are you? You look well.'

'I'm fine.'

'Good.'

He also ignored the rain.

'I'm still Dr. Chris's house-guest, you'll notice. The painters haven't finished slopping paint all over my books and now they've done the ceiling the wrong colour and it has to be done all over again,' he said. 'I'm taking Chris out to supper. Why don't you come too? I'm sure he'd like it as much as I would.'

'It's very kind of you but I have to go home. Dad has some people coming,' I lied.

'Oh. Okay. Come in and have a drink anyway,' he said, opening the front door. In the hall we passed the blonde Hendrika, who smiled at us and muttered something incomprehensible.

Ben and I went up into the sitting-room, the door opened and Hendrika came in. She said:

'The doctor will be out immediately.'

When the door closed we both laughed.

'I love Hendrika. Yesterday she told us supper was ready by coming in and announcing 'I'm all right'.' Ben paused. 'It's nice to see you, Candida.'

There was another pause.

'I haven't seen you because I've been working on my medical piece,' he said.

I had not asked him why he hadn't seen me; it was a male trick that always annoyed me. Did women give away so pathetically their desire to have men around that the males must make excuses all the time? I asked what medical piece.

'Didn't I tell you? It's been handy staying with Chris. At the fountainhead, so to speak. I'm doing a lid-off doctors. Private, group practice, the lot. Their image is slipping, you know. Quite nasty they are sometimes, too. Yet the poor things are disgustingly over-worked. I've found group practices with ten thousand patients. That's no joke, is it? You're lucky to have old Chris. Let's have a sherry. I gave him the bottle so I dare say I can help myself.'

He poured us out large glassfuls and drank his with evident pleasure, saying, 'Yes, it's the right kind isn't it?' Then he said, 'Chris will be hours, he's always late. Tell me all about you. Are you sure I can't persuade you to

113

have dinner with us?'

'I really can't.'

'Pity. Still, you can get dry,' he said, switching on the electric fire and moving it so that it shone on Sheba and me. The dog and I both began to steam slightly.

Ben leaned back in the old leather chair and looked over at me as if we were old friends.

'How's the will-power going?'

It was only then that I realised he didn't know about my decision. 'I'd forgotten! I meant to tell you when I saw you in the road just now. I'm going to do the play after all.'

He burst out laughing. 'I knew you would,' he said.

'But you advised me to stand firm!'

'No I didn't. I said you could stand firm if you wanted to. What I didn't say was that it was obvious you'd give in in the end.'

'Annoying of you to be right. How did you know?'

'Your father and you are not very evenly matched.'

'It wasn't like that at all,' I said, shifting.

He smiled, this time without laughing. He was attractive when he smiled.

'How did he persuade you?'

'You'll think it sounds stupid.'

'I certainly won't since it succeeded so well.'

'It sounds stupid.'

'Candida, don't be coy. Come on, I'm interested. How did your father get you to change your mind?'

I didn't answer for a moment. I saw again my father's face, and the way he'd wiped it over with his hand.

'It was when he started to talk to me, about my acting. I couldn't refuse him. It would hurt him too much. And I don't mean that in a conceited way,' I added, and Ben said: 'Oh you earnest old thing!'

He was watching me.

'What about your lost nerves? Did your decision restore them?'

'I haven't started working yet. I'm not going to worry about it until I do.'

'Or until you're in bed with a cold because you go for walks and get dripping wet. Take off your shoes and dry your feet by the fire.'

It wasn't difficult to turn the conversation back on to Ben. He returned happily to his lid-off the medical profession. He was in the middle of a long story about an interview with one of the men 'behind' the B.M.A. when Dr. Laurie came in.

Ben sociably waved his glass of the doctor's sherry.

'I found her in the rain. Her and the dog. I didn't really know which was Candida, they were both dressed in black and both wringing wet,' Ben said.

'I'm glad you look so well, child,' said Dr. Laurie. 'A little thin. Has your father been dieting you as fiercely as he does poor Tamara? I will have some of my sherry too, please, Benjamin.'

The doctor sat down in an old-fashioned red chair where I had seen him sit a hundred times. I smiled at him. Shrewd old fox. He was a tall, thin man, withered like a leaf in winter, his grey hair, once blond, crinkled on top of a balding head, his eyes, once bright blue, lined with red veins. He was facetious in a slow, droll way and made jokes that seemed to be for his own satisfaction rather than his patient's. He understood humanity alarmingly well. He teased Ben about his piece on doctors, saying he now had to watch every word he spoke. 'I shall be glad when he goes back to his own home even if I do have to buy the sherry. He times it carefully to catch me at the end of a rather long day and then asks me loaded questions like a barrister in court.'

'What kind of questions?' I said.

'A lot of very silly ones, my child. Would I say doctors kill more patients than they cure. Do we use you as guinea pigs. Do we understand modern drugs. Do we *like* our patients. I hope, my child, he hasn't been asking *you* any silly questions.'

'Oh come, come, I'm not grilling Candida. She'll throw me over if I do.'

'Has she taken you on, then?' inquired the doctor.

Ben asked me again to come out to dinner and the doctor joined him, but though the attention of two males was warming I still refused. In any case if Ben really wanted to see me he could ring. Better to go while I still seemed to be doing rather well.

Dr. Laurie kissed me good-bye and Ben drove me up the hill to the front gate. We stopped and listened to the rain drumming on the car roof. It was cosy in the wet dark.

'When am I going to see you? I miss you,' he said suddenly.

If you hope a man is going to say this, it is a kind of sexual pleasure when he does.

'Come to Tam's first night,' I said. 'My father always takes a load of V.I.P.s and it's such hard work. One is practically working during the performance. It's much more fun to go with just one friend. Do come. I'd love you to.'

'I'd like it too. Thanks.'

We seemed to have nothing more to say. We smiled at each other foolishly.

'Do you want a written promise that I won't be a journalist when I come with you?' he said at last.

'Yes please.'

'Are you going to tell your father who I am? He may know my name.'

I was just going to say that Dad didn't know the names of any journalists but those of a couple of critics (whose notices he said he never read), but I thought better of it. I murmured that Dad was always too busy at first nights to notice me. This simply was not true, but it would do for the time being.

When we said good-bye he pressed my hand. We looked at each other again and I wondered what it would be like if we kissed. I wasn't going to know this evening, anyway.

★ ★ ★

I was in bed next morning, listening to the radio, when Mrs. Brown tapped on the door and came in. This was a surprise, since her latest habit was to thrust only her head round the door.

This morning the whole body came in. She was very white and looked as if my father had been chewing her up again, although it was scarcely eight a.m. She was wearing a leather skirt and cowboy jacket of fringed leather; the cowboyish clothes sometimes emphasised her air of downtrodden romance.

'I am sorry to disturb you so early, Miss Waring, but Sir Robert says could you come down to his study? As soon as possible, I'm afraid.'

'To hear is to obey,' I said, jumping out of bed.

Mrs. Brown stood watching me. I caught her eye.

'Don't tell me. Let me guess. Dad instructed you to see that I washed and was fully clothed before being admitted to the presence. Did he perhaps say that No Child of His should walk around Half Naked?'

Mrs. Brown blushed. She hated jokes about Dad, and was particularly put out if Tam or I correctly quoted him since this showed insight (which she wished was hers alone) into the mind of God.

I showered, put on slacks and a darned Irish sweater that had once belonged to my father, and came down the stairs two at a time. The die was cast. If I was a flop, at least I would have tried. And since I was doing it for Dad as well as myself, I supposed I would be slightly supported. I tried to put out of my mind the cold shoulder he'd given me, frozen as meat in a deep freeze, in New York.

In the study ministered to by Mrs. Brown

he was at his desk like the Chief Druid with some attendant female priest. Opened letters lay around. Play scripts, heavily annotated, were spilling off a nearby chair. There was a toy-sized model of the Ghilain set on a shelf and some costume designs in a large artist's folder. A breakfast tray — orange juice, a boiled egg and nothing else — lay on the window-sill.

My father glanced up. To-day, wearing a washed-out blue windcheater and patched jeans, he looked thirty. When he saw me his face blazed as if a brilliant spotlight was suddenly switched on.

'There you are. Give your father a kiss!'

I threw my arms round him and we hugged. I loved kissing Dad, who smelled of eau-de-Cologne and sometimes of cigars.

Over my shoulder he roared:

'Mrs. Brown! Leave those letters *exactly* as I placed them.' Then, to me, 'I expect you're hungry.' Then, over my shoulder again, 'Mrs. Brown! To the kitchen, and ask Harriet to do bacon and eggs for Candida but no toast! At once, please. Leave that' — majestically indicating the telephone which had started to ring — 'My child will answer it!'

Mrs. Brown looked longingly at the telephone and left the room.

I picked it up obediently.

'Bobbie? It's Silas! I thought you were damn' well coming over to Athens this week!' cried a voice, over a rising and falling noise like the sea.

'Hallo, Silas. It's Candida.'

My father, who was standing listening with his hands on his hips, threw his huge eyes to heaven and staggered towards the settee with a broken leg. He looked like Long John Silver, a character I sometimes thought he resembled. Before I could interpret that performance into the telephone he shook his head, changed his role and indicated a burning pain in his stomach: an ad. for stomach powder, perhaps?

'Dad's not here . . . ' I was playing for time. 'He's upstairs . . . ' He changed again, clutching his jaw, and began to tie his face up with a handkerchief: a joke post-card of a man with toothache.

'He's having terrible trouble with a wisdom tooth.'

Approving nods from Dad.

'The doctor says he mustn't travel. He's taking antibiotics.'

'Good grief, how awful!' cried Silas, his voice coming and going. 'I had no idea — '

'Didn't you get our cable?' I asked, adding verisimilitude.

Ironic noiseless applause from my father.

No, said Silas, he hadn't received the cable. (I wasn't surprised.)

'How odd. Mrs. Brown sent it,' I replied disloyally.

'I must get Cables to trace it,' cried Silas. He returned ominously to my father's tooth. What did the dental surgeon say? What chance was there of Dad being allowed to come to Athens? 'Every day matters!' he cried.

My father scrawled on a piece of paper, and held it up to me. It said cryptically: 'Tell him I've got a way of getting Eric after all!'

I repeated this. There was a fascinated response from Silas. How did I know? Had I seen Eric? (I did not know who Eric was.) What had Dad got in his mind? I parried as best I could and arranged for Silas to call Mrs. Brown later in the day after Dad had seen his dentist.

'Bravo!' said Dad, when I had rung off. 'I'll sack Mrs. Brown and you take the job at half the pay.'

'Heartless beast.'

'So I am, so I am,' he said, laughing and showing his teeth.

While I ate breakfast, Dad roved round the room, picking up papers and putting them down. He read aloud a paragraph from one of the new plays and dropped it again. He looked over at me.

'Tt. Hurry up, child.'

I began to pour more orange juice.

'Not another drop. Come and sit by me.'

There was a hard-backed settee by the window, covered with green taffeta. My father sat down, patting a place beside him. He had *The Cherry Orchard* in his hand. It was the moment I had longed for and dreaded. Years ago when we were small children, we had been for autumn holidays by the sea. The water was cold in that English sea and I had dreaded swimming in it. Dad used to run across the sand. One moment he'd be running fast over the ribbed sand and rocks and long trails of slippery brown wrack, with me behind him, and then we'd be in the freezing, gripping water.

My father opened the book. He did what actors often do, using physical touch to make another person react, the artist's equivalent of the kiss of life. He put out his arm and pulled me close, pressing me to him. We sat huddled together, the book between us.

'You will be ready to play this part when you can talk about the character for an hour without stopping. Talk about her as if she is *yourself*. How well do you know Anya? How deeply have you thought of her? How much do you understand her?'

He spoke about Russian life at the turn of the century; of the sunset of the old-fashioned Tsarist era; of the graces and traditions that were dying in the old house with its spreading orchard in white flower. He talked about Anya, and what it felt like to be sixteen years old in Russia then. To be beautiful and, even with a family of improvident leftovers from the past, to be strong and happy. He talked about his own role, Anya's uncle Gayev, sweet-natured, kindly and doomed.

Time went by and Harriet came in with coffee. We drank it, but I never saw her go. Time went by and Mrs. Brown came in. My father waved her away.

We came to the end of the play, and the sound echoing through the orchard like the breaking of the string of the heart.

Dad shut the book with a snap.

'That'll do for now. Mm. You look pale.'

He pinched my cheek as he pinched Tam's.

The French clock on the mantelpiece struck fussily: one o'clock.

'Gentle heaven! I was lunching with François Poliakoff half an hour ago. Mrs. Brown!'

His huge voice shook the room. The door opened by magic. She had been standing on the other side.

'Ring Claridge's and ask them to tell Mr. Poliakoff that I shall be a few minutes late.'

'I have already done so, Sir Robert.'

The answer annoyed him. His black brows met in a solid bar.

'Go and order the car, woman.'

'It's at the door.'

He waved her out of the room. She left meekly, not surprised that her efficiency was ill received. I was sure she was still standing on the other side of the door.

He yawned and stretched, muscular as the panther he sometimes resembled. I yawned too. My eyes felt out of focus; I was shaking slightly. I was very tired. It was nearly five hours since we had sat down on the settee.

'Well?' said my father, with his comedian's look. 'Aren't you fortunate that you have ME?'

# 6

Mrs. Brown stood sentinel. She tried not to look at her watch.

'All right, all right,' said my father (she had not spoken a word). 'I'll take you with me, Candida. I shan't be a second, I must change my clothes.'

'But Dad!' I wailed.

'What is it *now*?' He stopped, one foot already on the stair and an expression of heavenly patience on his face, Saint Stephen just before the arrival of the boulders, holy martyrdom suffered for family.

'Dad! You don't want me to lunch with you, *please*!'

Lunches with Father and distinguished friends were Tam's and my most hated events. He made us work so hard.

'I do not. You have not met Poliakoff. He is woman-mad. One look at you, and he won't eat, let alone manage a sensible remark about his production. It will be leers and Magyar compliments. I am dropping you at the theatre. I've arranged for you to have voice-production, starting to-day. It needs work, that little pipe of yours.'

A moment ago he had regarded me with the sympathetic concern that Dr. Laurie or Ben might have, noticing that I was tired and trembling. Now I was to work on for hours.

'Come along, come along. You'll have to find your leotards too. You're going to gym this afternoon and those jeans are too tight. I shall be ready faster than you.' He darted up the stairs.

The Rolls dropped me off in a street near the Royalty, and Dad waved as the car moved into curdled lunchtime traffic. It was going to take him at least twenty minutes more to get to Claridge's. Poliakoff's stomach would be rumbling. It was fortunate that Mrs. Brown, waiting until my father was out of earshot, had telephoned once more to say 'Sir Robert will be another half-hour. Please apologise to his guest.'

Dad hated a realistic estimate of time when he had decided not to hurry. Reminders of minutes ticking by were forbidden. If he judged something deserved his punctuality, he would arrive on the hour: for rehearsals, for instance, or for Speech Days when we were children. But the majority of people who arranged to meet him had to be philosophical, since, as he would often exclaim, 'Am I not worth Waiting For?' His other favourite maxim was, 'It is a question of who is boss, Time or Me.'

At the Royalty, the lady who taught voice-production was waiting for me. We settled down to work. 'We must see about some food for you,' she said vaguely. But she forgot because she was sixty and lived on tea and devotion to the drama.

I had been right when I likened my return to the theatre to running into an autumn sea. For the next few days the water was freezing cold. It was a year since I had acted in New York, months since I had finished at R.A.D.A. The gentle routine of art school, of drawing in the old nursery, of going out with friends, vanished.

I was given gym lessons, voice-production, fencing (for balance), more voice-production. I was sent to join the Royalty mime school. My muscles, face, arms, neck, ached as I learned to indicate grief and joy without a word.

My father sent for me one morning when Harriet was with him. He looked me over and then spoke to her:

'Candida must lose five pounds. She looks too healthy. I want her face bonier, more refined. She must be a little aristocratic.'

'Five pounds in how long?' Harriet asked impassively.

He shrugged: 'A week.'

The diet that followed was worse than Tam's, it was that of a hermit. Dry toast; skim milk; meat and lettuce leaves. My father, meeting me in the garden, pinched the top of my shoulder to see how the diet was going. I said I felt like a horse.

'A race-horse,' corrected Dad.

I saw little of Tam, who was rehearsing all day and often late into the night. The final dress rehearsal of the Ghilain, the night before the opening, broke at four in the morning.

It rained all that day, summer rain, drenching and fresh-smelling and sad. When I came home after lunch I was tired and damp. I had spent hours in the gym, doing exhausting exercises that made my muscles scream, and later had been given lessons in dancing a Russian mazurka.

Up in the old nursery I found Tam on the floor hunched on the piggy rug. Her arms were round her knees. Rain pattered steadily on the skylight.

'I've been hanging from the parallel bars,' I said.

'Yeah,' said Tam, staring at the floor. She hadn't heard what I had said. Her face, white from sleeplessness, was covered in cold cream and shone greasily. Her hair was cruelly skewered into out-size rollers.

'I'm no good. I'm going to be awful to-night.'

I climbed the rocking-horse and set it creaking to and fro.

'Actors always think that.'

'No they don't. Some think they're going to be brilliant.'

'Maybe the seasoned ones. You're only starting.'

'Finishing, you mean,' she said inevitably. 'I'm just not funny. Why did I ever think I was?'

It was no good comforting, encouraging, or praising. She could not hear. There comes a time when only the opinion of the director or players in the actual production mean anything: only those involved know what they are talking about.

'What does Dad say?'

'That I've got to be on my toes. Ha, ha. I'm flat on my back.'

The rocking-horse creaked again. It needed oiling.

'You've got to *be* funny,' Tam said drearily. 'In your bones. Like Dad.'

She looked drained. That was what happened when you had been rehearsing too hard; you used up the juices.

'I haven't had the chance to tell you,' I said, raising my voice to penetrate the near-impenetrable egotism of a worried actor. 'I'm bringing a new man to your first night.'

It worked, she unclasped her hands from round her knees, and looked at me with eyes beginning to focus.

'Do I know him?'

I rode the horse backwards and forwards and said casually: 'Ben Nash.'

She actually looked interested. She had slightly projecting teeth, and with her mouth open she reminded me of an animal. A beaver, say. A russet-coloured beaver.

'The one with the hair? Came to Camden Town?'

'You sound surprised,' I said.

She was reviving.

'I should think you've met your match there.'

'What can you mean?'

'You do sound like Dad!' she giggled slightly. 'You even drop your jaw in the same way. You're getting more like him every day.'

'Tam, you are a master at avoiding the point,' I said, exasperatedly forgetting I had started the conversation to amuse her. 'Why have I 'met my match' with Ben Nash? I asked him because he's a nice man, and Dad's got the usual V.I.P.s coming and you know how stuffy it always is. I'd much rather enjoy your play with Ben.'

My sister stood up and groaned that every bone in her body was sore. She staggered over and sat on my drawing-table, putting her plump bottom on the sketches which had been left there for days.

'He's quite attractive,' she conceded, 'in a vulgar kind of way.'

'What on earth does that mean? Vulgar! You sound like a middle-class housewife in the nineteen-twenties. The only men we know are Johnnie, who's mad anyway, and a lot of gibbering actors with their egos showing. Ben's a human being.'

She yawned. 'I must go to bed. Dad said two full hours with the curtains drawn. 'Bye, darling. It's a comfort to know there's going to be one human being in the house to-night!'

She went off, quite pleased with her feeble joke.

For the first time for days I had a few hours off. This was not because my tyrannical father thought I needed it, but because there was no time for classes. The rehearsal rooms were empty. The Royalty had begun to prepare for to-night's opening.

Dad, who did not approve of leisure, had reminded me this morning that there were two books on Tsarist Russia I must study.

'You'd better look slippy and mug them

up to-day,' he said.

'I'll take them up to her room,' began Mrs. Brown.

'What! Can you spare the time to wait on a pack of teenagers when I need you!' cried my father. 'Let them run about after themselves.'

He often reminded us that we must 'run about' after ourselves. He could not bear us to be waited on. He would send us to the top of the house to fetch unnecessary things to see 'if our characters were in training.'

Dad had been poor as a boy. He enjoyed describing himself, a puny child of eight, going to the cellar at the bottom of the garden to fill enormous coal-buckets. His task had been to tend the kitchen boiler for his mother. His father, a clerk with no ambition but a passion for theatre and ballet, had filled Dad with the desire to act, and helped get him to drama school. Dad spoke with relish about the past. What a pathetic child he had been, with his clothes carefully darned and the recurring ear-ache which continually kept him away from school. He would describe his prowess on the football field — four goals! — then more ear-ache and no money for books. This memory of his parents' genteel poverty, with the necessity for doing every-thing for himself, convinced Dad of the impossibility of treating anyone as a 'servant', a word we simply never uttered. Dad would bully Mrs. Brown into splitting headaches, have inspiriting rows with fellow directors, terrorise his chauffeur, and lecture Harriet at the top of his voice if there were a mark on the carpet. Yet he firmly believed himself the most democratic man alive. Perhaps because he lived in the theatre, still often disordered and 'Bohemian' after hundreds of years, he kept a rigid order. Things must be well run and well done. He could not bear a dirty mark, a missing button, forgotten thanks. Everybody must work to keep things the way he demanded them. His memory was unfailing. 'Tam, did you have that buckle altered? Harriet, I want the carpenter to build me some shelves, David has a sketch of them exactly as I want them. Candida, have you written to thank that Danish man for the books he sent you? I asked you to do that yesterday.' Mrs. Brown wasn't allowed to bring me a book. I must go for it on my own two feet.

The house was quiet that afternoon. As I went along the passage I passed Tam's room, thinking she was certain to be asleep. She always had the trick of sleeping if Dad told her to do so. 'Take half an hour's sleep before the party, Tam!' he would say, or, 'For one hour before I come back to collect you, miss,

134

you must sleep.' Tam would crawl obediently between the blankets, shut her eyes, and fall asleep. 'She's Trilby,' Dad said to me, 'and I'm Svengali.'

I went along the passage to his study. The settee where we had sat by the window this morning still had the imprint of my father's back against a cushion and on it was the Russian knife he'd used to point out passages in the play.

I picked it up and put it back on his desk, glancing out of the window. Sheba was roaming on the lawn, looking for visiting cats.

The books in the study were on shelves built up to the ceiling on two sides of the room. A pair of library steps was in the corner. I pulled them out and climbed up to the Russian authors on the top shelf. There was a long row of them: hard-backed copies of classics, commentaries, paperbacks, an old-fashioned edition of *War and Peace* I had read as a schoolgirl. I stretched out to get the books and just as I took hold of them I heard a sound which made me almost fall from the steps. It was a long threatening snarl.

I steadied myself and looked into the garden and there was Sheba, completely still. Her rippling body was stiff, the hair stood up. Her lip was back and she was showing her long teeth.

Just as I started to climb down Harriet darted into my line of vision, seized Sheba roughly by the collar, and ran off.

That was odd. When did Harriet ever run? Who was Sheba growling at? She was a dog who never did anything but bark majestically. The only time I had known her to growl had been when I had sprained my ankle. Ventura had put ice on the swelling, I'd groaned aloud, and Sheba, under the impression Ventura was hurting me, would have bitten the girl's hand if I hadn't stopped her.

I picked up the books and went towards the kitchen. Down the passage I heard again a long, threatening snarl.

'Sheba! What is it, you fool!' I pushed open the kitchen door.

Sheba was standing in the middle of the kitchen, stiff with menace, Harriet's hand on her collar. As Harriet glanced up, I saw that her face was as grey as her hair.

Watching us was a burly man of about forty, with a yellowish face, black hair curling at the edges. His expression, supposed to be a smile, was a grimace.

'Miss Candida Waring in person!' he said.

'Jack Swift,' said Harriet without explanation.

'I knew you as a baby, Miss Waring.' He put out his hand and shook mine, 'I know all the greats. You name 'em, I know 'em.'

I did not answer but looked at Sheba again. Her fur had settled, but when she looked at the visitor she showed the whites of her eyes.

'I don't like dogs and they don't like me,' Jack Swift remarked.

'Could you take her with you, Candida?' Harriet cut in. Apparently she didn't trust the dog not to take a piece out of her visitor's leg.

'Okay.'

I bent to grasp Sheba's collar and my hand touched Harriet's. It was like ice.

She gave me a 'get-the-hell-out-of-my-kitchen' look. I pulled Sheba with me.

I thought over Harriet, and the visitor, and Sheba's behaviour, while I was dressing for the theatre. Harriet's reserve was quite unbreakable: useless to ask who the man was unless she decided to tell me. I did know she had disliked him. I hadn't fancied him myself.

Giving up the problem, I concentrated on the way I looked. A number of Tam's clothes and mine were based on theatre designs made by friends in the theatre wardrobe. They were original, and always interested my father. To-night I was wearing a dress similar to one from his production of *Troilus and Cressida*: it was ankle-length, cinnamon-coloured, clinging in Greek folds. Over it I wore the sable jacket he had given me. Tam and I had both been given furs after he'd made a Hollywood epic last year. He often gave us presents after a big success, and the gifts had the names of plays and films. Tam's moonstone bracelet was 'the Pericles,' my sable was 'the Brontë.'

Ben Nash had telephoned earlier to say that he would pick me up at seven o'clock.

'I'll be in the car at your gate. I won't come to the house.' Apparently he guessed I would be relieved by this arrangement. There was still the problem of saying who he was. And Dad was not at his best just before curtain-up: if he was acting, he was shut off by intense nervous concentration; if, as now, he was the play's director, his withdrawal was only a shade less complete.

There were voices coming from the drawing-room and I thought the door might fly open and someone call out to me, but that did not happen. Relieved, I reached the front door to see Ben's car already waiting. I ran through the rain. He looked boyish in a dinner-jacket that was slightly too tight.

'You're in beautiful time!' I said.

'You *look* beautiful,' he replied. 'A sort of dream,' he added unselfconsciously.

The pavement outside the theatre and the steps and foyer were crowded. Ben dropped me at the front of the house and drove off, saying heaven knew where he'd park and he'd find me near the box office.

'Don't let someone steal you.'

In the foyer were jostling people and the hot glare of TV lights.

Charles Lewis, a TV commentator I knew, came up. He was balding, with a knocked-about face. He was one of the few TV people my father liked and I was willing to bet that was why they'd given him the job to-night.

'Miss Waring. Please?'

The crowd eddied away, moved by one of those young men in TV teams: harassed equerries. Someone said to Charles Lewis: 'You're on,' and the commentator turned as if he had only just caught sight of me. His manner changed, became four times the size:

'Good evening Miss Candida Waring, can you spare us a moment or two? I'm sure the viewers will want to know how your family feels about this new production. Isn't it the first time your young sister Tamara has acted with the Royalty company?'

He'd got it wrong. They sometimes did.

'It's an exciting night for her,' I said (tactfully, I thought).

'What does Sir Robert feel about his daughter's chances?'

'He's always cautious.'

'What about you, Miss Waring? You acted in New York with your father last year. When are you going to join your father and sister in a play? Are we going to have another theatre dynasty?'

'You'll have to ask my father. We do as we're told!' I laughed because Dad had said at breakfast:

'If the TV lot ask you about yourself, say nothing. *I* will do the talking.'

'Thank you very much, Miss Candida Waring.'

Charles Lewis and I moved out of camera. He took my hand and squeezed it, muttering thanks rather as if I'd given him a present.

A moment later Ben came shouldering through the crowds. He was rather taller, certainly bigger, than most people. He kept out of the glare, in the centre of which the commentator had advanced towards my father, now arriving in the foyer.

'I'll bet that's going to be on the news and I shan't see my girl on the telly,' said Ben.

'They'll cut me out anyway. Dad was just behind.'

'Are you kidding?' Ben said in my ear. 'Candida, Candida, I don't know how you've stayed so self-effacing and I fear it cannot last.'

Our seats were in the front row of the

circle, at a merciful distance from Dad, who, taking his seat, created the same stir as royalty. He had eight people with him, and I muttered to Ben, 'Don't look or he'll beckon.' We stared intently at the stage (there was a curtain to-night — often the plays did not have one) while Ben told me some idiotic story to make me laugh. He was close to me, our shoulders touched.

The play started. It sparkled at once. My father had directed it fast, it had an aura like an early Chaplin movie, but a movie about the rich instead of the poor. Situations chased each other as the characters did, in the enchanting costumes of 1900 Paris. But what of Tam? I felt depressed because she was never quite light or quite funny enough. She looked so pretty. But her lack of technique showed, and as I watched I tried not to think that her performance to-night was a warning. I tried to shake off the uneasy superstitious feeling as I saw my pretty, pert sister down there on the bright stage.

When the play ended, the applause broke out fast before the curtain fell. It rose, fell, rose again. Periandra was given a special round. Tam won some friendly applause. Then the curtain rose once more, and there was Dad incongruous in dinner-jacket, a man in a mass of painted actors.

He stepped forward. I heard that noise I'd known since childhood, the deep-throated roar of the animal that loved him.

Ben and I walked slowly back to his car, which was parked in a side street off Covent Garden. The strong smell of oranges gave a peculiar feeling to the street, like the scented alleyways in Grasse.

He did not start the car right away, but turned towards me, saying he'd enjoyed the play so much and he must thank me for taking him. 'And to Sir's party, too!'

His manner, naïve, a boy convinced he's going to have a good time, gave me a pang.

'I hope you're going to enjoy the party,' I said. 'They're pretty much on one note, as you must know. Theatre people are such egomaniacs.'

'Not all.'

'Actors have to be. Have you known many?'

'One or two.'

'There'll be at least eighty at the party, all talking shop, all expecting you to know who they are and what they're playing and all being hurt if you don't. I expect if you're truthful you can't stand actors. Why should you? I don't blame you.'

He leaned forward and kissed me.

I had felt a tension between us all evening

and every now and again we touched by accident. But the kiss was unexpected. I had been kissed so often and usually knew when the kisses were coming and some were meant and others were not. Actors had taken me into dark gardens and the wings of theatres and pressed me close. Now and again I had wanted more than just kisses, but somehow my things with men always seemed to peter out. The actors were often swept off by Father, who, as he joyfully told me, was the one they really had their eye on anyway. I'd laughed, and my disturbed desire had died.

Kissing Ben wasn't any of that. Like the orange-smelling street, the kiss had a flavour peculiarly its own. We kissed for a long time. I shut my eyes and when I opened them I saw that his were closed, and to see him as gone as I had been was moving. When we separated, his face didn't look humorous or ingenuous any more.

'Ben.'

I leaned against him.

'You're very beautiful,' he said thoughtfully.

'I want you to think so.'

'And very sweet.'

'I'm not. But please believe it.'

'And too famous for me.'

I pulled myself out of his arms.

'What do you mean?'

'What I say,' he said, unconcerned by my angry voice.

'I'm not famous *at all*. That's ridiculous.'

'Come here, Candida,' he said, and put his arms round me again.

★ ★ ★

My father, who did not like parties, often gave them for his company. He said actors liked to be together so that they could complain. And anyway they were always hungry and it was nice to see them eating heartily.

There was music coming from the dining-room when we arrived: it was a local beat group, hammering at piano and drums, twangling with a sitar. Mozart was rippling from the drawing-room, and the two sets of sounds met and fought in the hall, with Mozart losing.

The actors in the farce had not yet arrived, they were still being kissed and admired in their dressing-rooms at the Royalty. My father never went round to do this. It was one of his rules that actors simply had to get used to: 'Sir doesn't.' Sir didn't, and Sir did not object to Tam and myself being let off the task of queueing to offer admiration. 'Just tell them later, and mind you do,' said Dad.

In the drawing-room, my father was with some people by the bar. He had his back to me, but inevitably knew when I came into the room, turned on his heel and beckoned imperiously.

I said, 'Come on, Ben. He wants us.'

'He wants *you*, Candida, off you go. You can leave me, I'm okay.'

I went unwillingly across the room.

Dad was with two of his close friends, men I'd known since I was a child. Clancy Carrington was a don who worked with Dad on Shakespeare productions. He was tall and stooping, with a huge black mole on his chin. He was clever and neurotically shy, never spoke to women unless absolutely forced to do so, and was now standing close to my father for protection against Periandra, who always tortured him by talk. The other man was James Delaval, a governor of the Royalty company, a showy lawyer and an M.P., who gave good performances in court and in the House. Dad liked Clancy for being a scholar and James for being a showman.

'Candida. More of a beauty every day,' said Delaval, kissing my hand.

'Good evening,' muttered Clancy, looking away immediately and putting both hands in his pockets.

Dad handed me a glass of champagne.

'Make it last. That's all you're getting.'

'For the whole party!' I wailed.

'Every single hour of it. Alcohol is forbidden. Do we inebriate our race-horses?' said Dad, who always came down heavily, at the slightest excuse, against drink for Tam and me. 'And who, pray, is that man who accompanied you to My theatre?'

My father was being the duke again. The role was one that he returned to with relish. He looked at me haughtily. I thought — I was always thinking — how beautiful he was.

'May I bring him over to meet you?' I asked with the deep respect the duke enjoyed.

'If you must.'

James Delaval looked over at Ben, who was talking to an elderly actress, drinking champagne and thoroughly at home.

'Surely that's Nash. One of the editors of *Pivot*, isn't he?'

I said yes and thought, 'That's torn it.' I waited with horrified interest to see what my father would do.

'Rather a good writer,' Delaval said patronisingly to my father, whose face was a deliberate blank. 'Works like a black' (dear, dear, mustn't say that!). 'Did a favour to the P.M., as a matter of fact' (lowering his voice). 'Wrote something that got in the American press about . . . ' His voice went even lower. My father, who had an interest in politics that began and ended with the subsidy given him by the ruling government, leaned forward to listen. Then, while I still waited for Jove's thunder:

'Bring him over, child.' My father waved at me, meaning 'I will grant an Audience.'

I returned to Ben.

'Dad wants to meet you,' I said.

I had said this often to actors and I was used to its effect. They tensed. They actually grew handsomer, more confident, cleverer: the chance of meeting my father made its own magic. But Ben, striding beside me in the dinner-jacket made for him when he was twenty, was undisturbed.

'This is Ben Nash. He's a friend of Dr. Laurie's,' I said.

'How do you do, Sir Robert,' said Ben, shaking my father's hand in the rather hearty firm way that was not unlike Dad's.

My father gave the famous smile which emphasised his high cheekbones, made his great eyes shine. How well I knew that smile. Dad often seemed to me to be the only human being in the world who truly merited the description 'fascinating.'

James Delaval said: 'Hallo, Nash. Last time I saw you, you were coping with the P.M.'s temperament. Don't know how you could bear it!'

'I enjoy temperament, Mr. Delaval.'

My father said: 'That's what actors like to hear. Tell me, Mr. Nash . . . '

I moved out of the circle, so that my father could talk to Ben alone. He was censorious about our companions: Tam and I were used to criticism and questions. All the actors who took Tam or me around knew this and would exclaim, 'Help! Here's the Knight,' when Dad came into a room where they were dancing or flirting with us.

As I left Ben and my father together, there was a stir in the doorway. It was Periandra, dressed in gold, and another figure, small and plump. Tam.

I ran over, and, 'Oh Candy! Did I make you laugh?' cried Tam, catapulting herself at me like Sheba.

My father insisted on Tam and me being at all his parties and we were never allowed to go to bed until the last guest had gone, which meant until five in the morning. Many times I'd secretly gone to the kitchen to have black coffee to stop my eyes rolling with sleep. Parties of pro's were much of a muchness: everyone started brilliant, then grew emotional, finally we all found ourselves in an exhausted limbo from which it was impossible to move. Nobody ever seemed to go home. Many times I'd sat on the stairs at dawn with actors, soothing or listening to them, after a whole long night spent playing the role of looking-glass.

Ben, apparently, loved parties. He enjoyed talking to the company and had the trick of it. Even the most morose actors stayed with him, talking or watching the dancers. That was something actors did superbly — they danced like creatures in the jungle.

It was after four when the guests began to go, offering each other lifts home and still making jokes and kissing. Ben and I were in the study, the folding doors had been pushed back to connect it with the drawing-room. We were sitting on the library steps, while someone played 'The Teddy Bears' Picnic' on the piano in the drawing-room and someone else sang what sounded like a very rude version of the words.

'I must go, Candida. And you must get some sleep. Working to-morrow?'

'Like a slave.'

'Then off you go and get some rest.'

'No.'

I pressed my back against his knees.

'I understand why Sheba leans against people,' I said.

He laid his hand on top of my head.

149

'You're safe, Candida.'

'Am I?'

'You're loved. Your father loves you very much.'

'Oh, I know.' I turned round and lifted my chin to look up and he said:

'Don't look like that. It makes me want to kiss you.'

'I want you to.'

'Come along. Say good-bye to me at the door.'

The drawing-room was empty except for one young actor, still playing 'You're sure of a big surprise.' The candles which Harriet had lit hours ago were burned down to their sockets. The room smelled of scent and drink and cigars. We walked into the hall.

*Surely we'll kiss again?* I thought.

Standing by the door, springing and erect, was my father. He was with Periandra, who was winding a white woollen shawl round her head and shoulders.

'Good night, my darling Bobbie!' she crooned, putting up both arms and locking them round him.

'Good night, darling Peachey. Thank you for your performance.'

'You really liked it?' Just for a moment her face, framed in the white shawl, looked helpless and hopeful.

'Beautiful. A piece of Offenbach,' my father said.

They stood staring at each other. The same expression, loving, satisfied, lit their faces.

There was a thrilling pause.

Periandra suddenly yelled towards the open door:

'Dennis! Harry! Have you got the car?'

Obedient male voices chorused from the dark.

'Open the car door. You know how bad my rheumatism is. *I* am coming!' cried Periandra. With another swimming look at Dad, she swept out.

My father watched her go, and then turned; he'd already seen us without appearing to do so.

'Ah, Mr. Nash.' He had, of course, remembered the name though it had been spoken hours before when they were introduced. My father's prodigious memory touched people. He knew it.

'Thanks for the party, Sir Robert. It was kind of you to ask me,' said Ben. If a slight flicker of irony showed in my father's face, I hoped Ben didn't see it. 'And thank you for the play to-night. I'm sure it'll be a big success.'

'We do our best. Our humble best,' said my father.

The differences between the two men were very marked as they stood together. Dad's face, refined, bony, was a mask that could alter from Adonis to Macbeth, from camp humour into deep tragedy. Ben's face, fattish, humorous, was his own. It was not created from the souls of others.

'And you should be in bed, Puss!' said my father, wheeling on me. 'Work, that's for you from now on. We'll see if you can do as well as your sister.'

He turned his great eyes on Ben and hissed, 'We mustn't waste her time, hey?'

I scarcely had the chance to mutter good night before Dad had shooed me up the stairs.

★   ★   ★

I had been asleep two or three hours when I woke thinking I heard the telephone. It was seven o'clock, with a damp day beginning outside.

I lay still, thinking of Ben. A feeling came over me that I'd never known till now. It was the thing I'd read about, cried about in the theatre, heard other people rave about.

I got out of bed and tugged at the curtains to let in the grey morning. The bedroom door opened and Tam peered in.

'I thought I heard you. I kept hoping you'd wake.'

She came in slowly, wearing as usual my father's white bath robe which trailed behind her. It gave the impression of a christening robe or a shroud. She was very pale. She sat down on my bed and said nothing.

'You've read the notices!' I said, alarmed.

She nodded. 'I was sitting by the telephone for hours waiting, and as soon as it rang I snatched it off its hook so as not to wake Dad. Periandra was in Fleet Street with the boys. She read them all to me.'

'Well? well?' I was chilled with nerves. 'Didn't they like it? Surely it's a success?'

'Oh yes. They liked it. They were raves.'

I didn't need to ask but I had to. 'And yours weren't so good?'

Tam said brightly: 'They were kind. Bloody kind. Patronising and kind.'

'Where are they?'

'You'll see them soon enough,' she said irritably, 'and so will Dad, and you'll both go through them picking out the kind bits to cheer me up and in the end I shall begin to believe you're right and I'm okay.'

She looked very young.

'Tam.'

She gave my father's sardonic smile. 'I know what you're going to say because I've said it to people myself. Don't bother. I *wasn't* much good and I know I can do it if I try and I'm going to try. Let's get coffee.'

We crept down the passage to the nursery and made coffee, talking in whispers. No one in a house of actors talks in a normal voice until the most important player in the house is awake.

Tam tried to be fair over the notices of the other actors, and was genuinely happy that the play was a success. But running through her talk was the all-absorbing depressing thought of herself.

'Dad was worried about my comedy bits,' she said gloomily.

'Do you think he was right?'

'He's never wrong,' she said piously.

I laughed, annoyed to see her under the spell of Svengali.

After a while she roused herself, and managed to look at me as if noticing who it was.

'You fancy that Ben Nash character, don't you?' she said.

'Do I?'

'It showed. Periandra mentioned it.'

'Oh, Periandra. She's always looking for sex when two people have a drink together.'

'I think you ought to know Dad noticed it too.'

'What on earth does that mean?' I said.

She peered out into a world that this morning she was finding pretty dark and dangerous.

'I saw him looking at you and Ben Nash once or twice. It was easy to see what he was thinking.'

'But he can't dislike Ben!' I exclaimed, immediately remembering to lower my voice. 'He only met him last night,' I whispered angrily. 'And as for that corny old stuff about Ben being a journalist, it's pitiable.'

'He doesn't dislike him, Candy. He doesn't dislike my silly old Johnnie Buckingham, for that matter. He's just busy making us into actresses,' said Tam, the religion throbbing in her voice.

I looked at her. She was sad and flattened by anticlimax. She must have guessed she hadn't pulled it off last night. Seeing her fears confirmed and her work dismissed in the newspapers was a blow she was still feeling. Yet she still repeated, hushed, holy, 'That's what Dad is doing.'

# 7

Within forty-eight hours of the Ghilain success, Tam had a TV offer and Dad decided to go to Athens after all.

'And I can guess why he's changed his mind, Mrs. B.,' I said. I had called in to her office to hear the news.

'Sir Robert needs to go into the new film in depth. All he did at first was a preliminary survey. He wants to go beyond that. To disseminate the spectrum,' said Mrs. Brown, almost to herself. She had occasional fits of using language left over from commerce; I often thought it was a comfort to her. The old times.

'I suppose he weighed up the notices and decided he could take his beady eye off the Royalty for a bit.'

'Sir Robert gave the notices his attention.'

'Went through them with a microscope and a stethoscope, you mean.'

Mrs. Brown did not like her idol's daughters to be flip. She picked up a file on which my father had scrawled 'This and That.' It was his favourite file. 'File these women in This and That,' he would say. Mrs.

156

Brown hated that file and couldn't get used to it.

Tam came into the office wearing a bright green sweater with a polo neck, her hair shiny as a brass button.

'I thought I heard you gals. Hi, Mrs. B. How's the box office tinkling?' Tam recovered fast.

'Sir Robert says it is not too bad.'

'Not bad!' exclaimed Tam with all Dad's respect for money. She seized the clip of advance box-office takings from the desk before Mrs. Brown could stop her, and muttered to herself:

'Let's see. What's the figure for capacity?'

'Eight hundred and seventy-five pounds ten shillings a performance, miss, and what has it got to do with you?' said my father, coming into the room.

'Oh Dad! Every actress likes to know.'

'Every actress can mind her own business,' retorted my father, snatching the clip of papers from Tam and putting them behind his back. 'If junior members of My company start checking the figures, we're in for a nice future. A cast of computers. Mrs. Brown! Keep my children's hands out of the till. Gentle heaven, don't I feed you? House you? Nay, even employ you?' To-day we were no longer the duke's two daughters. We were nineteenth-century mill girls and lucky to get the jobs.

'Mrs. Brown!' My father rather liked sending the name echoing round the room like a battle-cry. 'Lock up the files. Candida! To my study, please.'

He went out of the room ahead of me, walking with a loping stride which swayed from the hips. I followed more slowly. I was feeling a little low, in spite of determined cheerfulness. I had not seen Ben for two days and didn't know when we were going to meet again. I wanted to think about Ben. And my father was going to talk about this morning's rehearsal. That hadn't been good either.

'Sit down, Puss,' said my father, pointing to a stool facing his desk.

He sat in the Roman Consul's chair, his hands automatically feeling for the wooden claws. Silence. Then, quick as a pouncing animal:

'What's up? What's wrong?'

'I don't know what you mean.'

'What's up? What is it?'

I was scared. I was faced with my father's intuition, radiating an unearthly prescience. Had he guessed, something that I scarcely knew myself, my uneasy attraction for Ben? Other girls might fool other fathers. The only way to evade him was with some kind of

truth. The rehearsal, for instance.

'Was I hopeless this morning?'

'Did you think you were?' he demanded.

'Yes.'

'Quite right. And don't excuse yourself by saying it was a first reading.'

'I wasn't going to.'

'Most actresses do.'

He lit one of the thin black cheroots he smoked sometimes and said conversationally:

'A first reading does not have to say nothing. Of course we all work differently, but take Periandra. She begins to set a performance from the first time she speaks her lines. You're flat. Now, now,' holding up his hand, 'we know you are not acting yet, but you sound to me as if you are not thinking either. Candida!'

For a second my eyes had strayed to the library steps in the corner where I had sat with Ben at the party and he'd put his hand on top of my head.

'Listen to me!' said my father dangerously.

'I am listening.'

'Then keep your eyes on my face. You know that when I speak as your Director you must do that. All the time. Are those steps of more interest than Me? Concentrate.' The cigar burned between his fingers, he wrinkled his eyes above the smoke. 'Remember. There's only one thing in the world worth doing. And I am teaching you to do it.'

* * *

He was leaving for Greece that afternoon, and he sent a message that Tam and I must lunch with him. My father often took his meals alone or ate while working with colleagues. Sometimes Harriet and the Italians walked in and out of the study all day, with successions of trays. Black coffee. Steak. Tea. Cake for visitors. Ryvita for Dad. But now and again he'd take a meal in the dining-room and command our presence.

When we arrived for lunch, Dad, in high spirits, offered us a feast of cheese, raw tomatoes, and his favourite drink, a yellowish soup of raw carrot juice which was disgusting. During the meal the telephone rang six times and Mrs. Brown darted in and out like a swallow building its nest. At one point the dining-room door opened and a six-foot-high horsehoe of white heather came in apparently by itself.

'Well, that's nice!' exclaimed Dad.

Above the quivering blossom and ribbon, Harriet's grey head and haggard face appeared.

'From the Caledonian Lovers of the Drama,' she said.

'You must always wear heather, Harriet. It suits you,' said Dad.

'You're not joking, of course,' she replied, dead-pan. She propped the hoop of flowers by the wall. He sipped carrot juice and smacked his lips as though over a vintage wine.

'What's up, Harry?' he said suddenly.

It was the identical pounce he had used on me. That and the other devilish habit, the rarely-used nickname. On chosen occasions I was 'Candy' or 'Puss.' Now and again, Harriet was 'Harry.' When he said it this time she flinched.

'Nothing's up.'

He continued to study her.

'Take a holiday. Do you good. Stop running about after those lazy daughters of mine.'

'I don't want a holiday,' was the sour reply.

'Go to the Danish Ballet School for a week. You know you like Solveig Halager and she's always asking you to stay. She wrote to me about you only a few days ago. Lots happening in Copenhagen just now. A new thing: a ballet where the scenery moves and the dancers don't. Like to see that, wouldn't you?'

161

'No thank you, Sir Robert.'

The horseshoe was in danger of slithering to the floor, and Harriet turned her back on my father and steadied the flowers against the wall. Dad crunched a stick of celery.

'Harry. Come here.'

Tam and I watched in silence. Mrs. Brown, jealous of Harriet's place in the family, fiddled with some papers. Harriet walked slowly towards my father. He put out a hand and grasped hers. They looked at each other.

'Harry, you're a fake,' he pronounced, and he kissed her hand. 'Off with you. To the Royal Ballet or the kitchen or wherever you choose. You always do as you like. You're the tyrant around here.'

He left the house after lunch, with the turmoil and bustle that always surrounded his leave-takings. He enjoyed making everyone hurry, particularly as *he* never did. If things were not heightened by urgency and drama he soon made them so. He finally strode down the path with Mrs. Brown trotting beside him in white suède and Garbo hat looking at her watch in horror. I quite expected Dad to put his head out of the car window and shout: 'Telephone the airport and tell them to hold the plane.' He'd done that before. He merely kissed us both, saying to Tam: 'Your exit last night was lousy again,' and to me: 'Periandra has been instructed to ring me and report on rehearsals. Don't imagine My eye is off you, Puss, just because I happen to be in Greece.'

The car drove away. Silence followed like a clap of thunder.

Tam and I trailed into the garden and lay on the lawn by the lavender hedge. Sheba came up and sat beside us.

'Candy,' said Tam, after a while.

I didn't answer. I was wondering where Ben was. Did one ring a man like that?

'What about Pop with Harriet at lunch!' said Tam. 'I believe he thinks she is in some kind of trouble. And so do I.'

I turned to my sister, feeling guilty and rather disgusted at myself. I was selfish. It was disgusting to be selfish. Ambitious tough little Tam wasn't. I said: 'I meant to tell you about the man who was with Harriet in the kitchen.' I told her the story. Tam was unsurprised.

'I've seen him too,' she said. 'Yesterday in the High Street with her. They weren't saying a thing, just walking together. Harriet looked like thunder. I nosily asked her later who he was. 'An *extremely* old friend,' she said, practically spitting.'

'But we must do something!'

My sister smiled.

'You are funny. Such a dasher-in with the

first-aid box. If you weren't an actress, I'd cast you as a nurse. Harriet is *forty-three*. How can we girls rescue her from the nasty man? You can bet your boots Harriet copes far better than we ever could. So don't go ringing that ambulance bell.'

'I'd rather help than not,' I said, discomfited.

'It's always easier to help than just to look on. What I want to know is, where did he spring from?'

I was relieved by her unconcerned manner. She was sometimes perceptive about people, just as she was sometimes tactless and snobbish.

'Perhaps he's a husband she left years ago,' I suggested.

'We'd have heard about *that* before now.'

'A love from the past, back from Australia and wants ready money?'

'Candy! We're not in the old silent movies!' said Tam. 'And what idiot would look for ready money in our house?'

She was right. Dad, generous with presents, enjoyed seeing us expensively dressed and commanded a home flowing with luxury, but couldn't bear to carry cash around with him. He liked everything settled by cheque. Until Tam had a pay packet when she started to act, and for the short time of

164

my New York work, we had to put everything we bought on one or other of Dad's many accounts, obtaining his lordly permission in advance. Harriet never had any money either. When Tam and I were children, the three of us pooled our money on the kitchen table before going to the films — scarcely scraping ten shillings together.

'Perhaps the man's an old friend who now bores her and we're making a fuss over nothing,' said Tam. 'Harriet's probably being dreary because of her age. Talking about the menopause, darling, Periandra was telling me all about it in the Green Room. She says it's frightfully good for an actress; I mean you get all gritty and irritable and sharp and you can use that, and then sometimes you get all vague and don't-care-ish and that's good too. Periandra says it's always useful to have a bit of mystery, even if it's glands. And then she says when the change is over your head goes crystal-clear. Like people feel after gout. I'm looking forward to it.'

'You have around thirty-five years to go yet.'

'Oh, it'll race by,' said Tam cheerfully. 'And then I can play all those roles, duchesses, and Cassandra, and bitches in Ibsen.'

We went back to the house. Tam disappeared on her own affairs. She had numbers of dates, her life was a complex pattern of arrangements. There were Indian films, dancing, jazz, club theatres, girl friends (Tam always had two or three actresses around). Voice-production and gym also had to be fitted in because Dad had left instructions about those.

Thinking how much I was going to miss Dad for the few days he was away, I had to return to the Royalty for another not-looked-forward-to rehearsal. I changed into practice clothes, black cotton sweater, leotards and gym shoes, and was coming down the stairs, *The Cherry Orchard* under my arm, when the telephone rang.

Harriet, who was in the hall, picked it up. Over her shoulder she said: 'Wait, it may be for you.'

'Harriet, it is *always* for Dad.'

'Want to bet?' she said, handing me the receiver.

'Candida? Ben. I've been trying to get you for days. You're very elusive. Will you have dinner with me to-night?'

I said I would like to. I felt my cheeks go red with relief and pleasure.

'I'll pick you up at the theatre,' he said. 'What time do you stop rehearsals?'

'I don't know. They sometimes drag on and sometimes finish early.' I was rather over-eager and I almost suggested coming to his office, when Ben said that he'd wait for me at the Ritz, okay? He'd sit and read his own paper until I came. 'I shan't worry if you're late, and you are not to either.'

I asked smilingly how he knew I would worry and he replied that never mind he did know. I went off to the Royalty delighted with myself and the day.

When Dad acted in a play as well as directing it, he always had a co-director. For *The Cherry Orchard* he'd chosen Gareth Owen, a clever temperamental Welshman, the head of the Royalty mime school.

This afternoon Gareth decided on a 'movement' rehearsal. 'Use your bodies. They're beautiful when they're used correctly,' he said. 'Have you seen the Berliner Ensemble? They move like acrobats. Come along, Candida; bend backwards from the waist, darling. Turn to Trofimov . . . remember, he's in love with you and you know it . . . Like this. Again. Periandra, move across there. That's a bit too stiff.'

'Charlotta's wearing whalebone!' said Periandra, sharply.

'Whalebone does *bend*, darling!'

'Does it?' drawled Periandra. 'Come and feel.' She slapped her waist; it sounded as if she were hitting a wall. She was already bound into the ferocious stays she would use under her costume as Charlotta.

During a break I sat with Periandra and her attendant men while she expounded about *The Cherry Orchard*. 'Did you know Chekhov used only to write four lines a day!' she exclaimed. 'That's why it's so perfect.' While she talked I saw Sid, the stage door keeper, come into the rehearsal rooms and over towards me.

'Pal of yours on the blower, dear,' he said.

Periandra stopped talking and looked at me, her eagle's face sharp with interest.

'Mr. Nash, I think it was,' said Sid. 'Says he's held up. Won't be able to make it till nine so perhaps you'd better cancel your date. He's holding . . . '

'I'll speak to him,' I said, jumping up.

'Back to your places, please!' cried Gareth Owen.

Periandra stood up. 'Candida! *What* are you waiting for? The director is calling. Tell whoever it is you cannot speak now,' waving Sid away as if he were a palace enunch.

'No, no, Sid; say I'll be with him at nine!' I shouted.

'Gentle heaven!' cried Periandra in my father's exact tone of sardonic disapproval.

The rehearsal was due to run until seven-thirty, but Periandra and three other members of the company were also playing in the Ghilain farce, so the director called another break to release them at six.

'Aren't you going to be hungry, Periandra?' I asked. 'You've got the whole of to-night's performance to get through.'

'I always give a performance on an empty stomach,' she replied witheringly. 'How little you still know.'

She was swathing herself in another stole — this one candy-floss pink, when a girl of about fourteen came hesitatingly into the rehearsal rooms. Periandra beckoned.

'Over here! Candida, I would like to introduce you to my niece. Floss, this is Miss Candida Waring.'

'How do you do.' The girl gave a quick smile and was immediately serious again. She was a round-faced girl, with freckles on the kind of nose I connected with comedy. Her hair, fiercely brushed and fiercely pulled into bunches, was blondeish brown. Her manner was reserved, either very shy or very self-possessed.

Periandra, arms folded, looked Floss over with the air of Queen Elizabeth, this time with a favourite maid in waiting.

'Floss has called to meet the boys in the Wardrobe and talk about theatre designs. She's already a brilliant artist and has sold four drawings,' she said, her actress's voice making every word a knockout.

Floss gave her aunt a look which Periandra missed.

'She has designed two dinner dresses for me. Wonderfully. She also makes gingham dolls and sells scores of them. She must make some for you and Tam. Give her an order now, they are fifteen shillings each,' said Periandra, waving at me as if I were younger than her niece.

Floss muttered something which sounded like 'Help.'

'Come along, child, don't *moon!*' exclaimed Periandra, 'Cliff is going to show you round the Wardrobe and tell you about cutting out buckram, so you must *pay attention.*'

The brilliant artist, docile as the deer she rather resembled, followed her aunt.

Five minutes later, just before rehearsal started again, Floss came running back, straight over to me. Her face was pink.

'Miss Waring! *Please* don't take any notice of Aunt Peachey. She's always on about my dolls and I only do them in the holidays and I know you don't want one!'

'But it might bring me luck, Floss.'

'No, no, it's one of Aunt Peachey's gags. I must go. I'm supposed to be back-stage. If

170

Aunt asks you, say I sold you the mauve one with the ketchup on it, that'll prove I've inherited her business head.' She ran out.

When the rehearsal finally ended I felt flat and tired. I went to the stage door to ask Sid what he'd said to Ben Nash and had Ben got it right.

'Sure he got it. You're meeting him at nine. Didn't sound too pleased at it being so late,' said Sid, looking over the sports page.

I went out into the street. It was theatre time; the crowds had already begun to collect in the foyer and to cluster on the pavement. I wondered if I would go and watch the opening scenes of the farce — I wasn't due to meet Ben for a long time yet. It was a habit at the Royalty for members of the company who were not playing to go up to the dress-circle sometimes and watch whatever play was on that evening. The actors who did this never commented, they just went up to the circle and stood in the dimness, silently joining the thing happening up on the stage. Theatre people find even a few minutes of a good performance refreshing: like paying a brief visit to a friend. But to-night I did not want to watch, and went into the street.

It was high summer and London was full of visitors carrying maps of the Underground. There were Scandinavians fair as butter;

Americans in silk mackintoshes; beautiful girls in saris with caste marks on their foreheads.

I went into the coffee bar facing the Royalty. Four or five of the company were there, eating spaghetti. They leaned on their elbows, talking intently. I knew that if I joined them I'd be welcomed — that is how pro's are. But just as I didn't want to watch the play on-stage, so I didn't want it off-stage either; I walked out of the coffee bar and slowly through the warm streets to Green Park.

It was crowded with people, enjoying the balmy night and the freedom of sitting in the open air on the dry grass. London was like a Spanish city. But the crowds who lay around were English crowds, close together and already surrounded by paper bags, for the English eat sweets when they are happy.

The stretch of sloping grass towards Buckingham Palace, which sometimes in the winter dark was deserted, wide and mysterious, looked small. Everywhere I looked there were lovers. They lay like pieces of fitting jigsaw, the law only just keeping them from making real love. Each boy had thrown aside his jacket and lay pressed against his girl, oblivious of everything else in the city. Every girl lay looking up at her lover's face and the sky. The air was full of pigeons flying in pairs, settling in the trees, their weight making the leafy branches slither and bounce.

I crossed the Mall into St. James's Park. It was beginning to grow dark and the water reflected a string of lights. Flocks of ducks quacked low, now and again setting off across the water, ripples trailing behind them. Along the grassy banks lovers lay here too, like felled trees.

Ben was waiting for me when I ran up the marble steps into the Ritz. He was at a little table, reading his own paper as if he'd never seen it before; he did not hear me come over, and when I said hallo he started.

'Candida!' He gripped my hands; we beamed as if we had not met for weeks. He was full of solicitude. How late it was — how good of me to come — he'd been worried but when he had tried to change our date the stage door keeper had only said something about my meeting him at nine and rang off. Ben had not liked to ring me back during the rehearsal. I must be tired! I must be hungry!

He shepherded me tenderly into the restaurant and ordered a meal, remembering that I was on a diet. 'Your father said you were allowed one glass of wine, didn't he?'

I noticed that something between us had changed — or rather, had advanced. We had settled for a pleasure in being together.

During the meal he talked, enjoying telling me all the things he'd been doing since we last met. He gave colour and detail to his stories, and when I sometimes interrupted or laughed he wouldn't be hurried. He said good-naturedly: 'Wait, I haven't come to that bit.'

Ever since I'd met him I had thought Ben ingenuous, and it is true that, compared to the wry chat of theatre people, Ben had a kind of simplicity. He was an optimistic charitable man, who preferred to think well of people. Perhaps this gave his writing and the way he worked a particular flavour. He was inquisitive and probing, and it fascinated him to bring stories to light; he was a journalistic detective. But in the end his conclusions, though tough and fair, were kindly.

He was also very sex-conscious, and I suppose I caught this from him; when we were together I felt it between us all the time.

We were having coffee at the end of the meal when he said: 'I hope you've noticed I haven't asked you about the play. Don't think I haven't wanted to. I thought you might prefer not to talk about it.'

'Yes. I think I'd rather not.'

He said quite right, quite right, talking about certain things dissipated them. 'And of course if I encourage you not to talk about yourself I get all the attention!' He added that food had done me good and I had colour in my cheeks again.

I said, 'My father used to say that, when he forced us to go out for freezing cold walks in winter. He'd stay by the fire reading and when we came home would admire our cheeks when we practically had frostbite.'

'I like a bit of paternal firmness. A few fathers are afraid of their daughters or mystified by them. They hide behind a male reserve. Is your father reserved?'

I laughed. There wasn't a piece of reserved country in the whole atlas of my father. There might be mountains down which you'd fall to break your neck or rivers you'd drown in. There were no fences. 'No. He's not reserved. He belongs to everybody.'

'Because he's an artist,' Ben said. 'Do you belong to everybody?'

'I'm not an artist.'

'Yet.'

The town was alive with cars and people when we drove home at midnight, but the hilly road at home was lonely. Lights shone down the slope, the houses behind high hedges were dark. Ben shut off the engine and pulled me into his arms. He looked down at me and I saw the expression I'd seen before, conscious, somehow marked. I could feel his heart pounding against my chest as if it were my own and when we stopped kissing my head swam. I waited for more kisses but his face altered back to its usual expression, ingenuous and impenetrable.

We walked down the path to the front door holding hands. He waited as I found my key. I turned to say good night, longing to be touched.

'Good night, little girl,' he said, patting my cheek as if I were fourteen.

\* \* \*

I thought of Ben the moment I woke up, and lay staring at the ceiling wondering why I felt dreary. I wanted to cry and that was pretty silly. It was horrible wanting to be more kissed, not being kissed. It made me feel hollow as if I were hungry.

There was a tap on the door and Harriet came in, carrying a breakfast tray.

'Mrs. Brown telephoned from Athens to say Sir is going to be out there three more days and you are to have halibut oil capsules,' said Harriet. 'Sir also sent orders that you are to be given breakfast in bed and why hadn't I gone on holiday. Like Alexander the Great, he commands his mighty kingdom from afar.'

176

She poured the coffee and took an egg-cosy off the boiled egg. The cosy, in raffia, had been made by Tam when she was six, and was discoloured and frayed. Harriet would never throw it away.

'What else did he say?'

'What he did *not* say was 'How is my elder daughter's sex life?' '

I buttered a piece of toast the size of a postage stamp, which was all my diet allowed.

'Are you going to tell, or am I going to cross-question?' said Harriet sitting on my bed, a thing she hadn't done for years.

'Nothing to tell. Not one damned thing.'

Harriet scratched her nose.

'So he hasn't fallen for you.'

'I don't know what you mean.'

'Don't be difficult, Candida. You're very taken with that man. Tam's full of it. Periandra came round for one of her 'kitchen chats' yesterday evening. She was full of it too. Very sharp about you 'tagging after a reporter' as she put it.'

'What else did Periandra say?' I believed in Periandra's sibylline qualities. She had eyes in the back of her head, like my father. 'Nothing else. She was on about her early life in the ballet. Ballet my foot! She danced twice in *Sylphides* at the age of twelve and she has bandy legs.'

'They're not her best points.'

'Oh, no no, my girl, you're not using Tam's gag, changing the subject,' said Harriet. 'Are you serious about Ben Nash?'

'I like him.'

'You're a rotten actress. Sir's quite right when he says you'll have to damn well work at it. I think that boy-friend of yours is upsetting you. Why?'

She did not appear to expect an answer but looked at the ground and sighed.

'That horse-shoe made of heather was delivered at the wrong house,' she said. When she walked across the room, I wondered why she moved as if it hurt her.

★ ★ ★

The early run-throughs were over and we were starting to work intensively at *The Cherry Orchard*. The cast, twenty of us, were at it ten hours a day. One morning before rehearsal I was asked to go to the Wardrobe to see Cliff Dexter, who was doing my costumes.

The Wardrobe was very cramped, and was situated in what had been the boxers' changing and locker rooms. Walls had been torn down and the place was now filled with trestle tables and the kind of wooden racks

178

which you expect to see filled with hay. Tables and racks were heaped with fabrics of dull or brilliant colours, with buckram, leather, jewels, buttons the size of saucers, scissors large as instruments of torture.

Cliff Dexter, a gnome in mauve jeans, was sitting on a step-ladder busily sewing. He was a wizened man of fifty with cornflower-blue eyes in a brown face, and white hair in a crew-cut.

'There you are. I want your measurements for Anya. Seen your designs yet? You have four changes. More than my ladies in Mozart. They were lucky to get two — even Susannah, and she was *brilliant*.'

Cliff had worked for years in an opera group, and compared everything in the opera to the drama's disadvantage.

He pointed to the wall facing him; it was covered with pinboard on which were fixed some *Cherry Orchard* costume designs. There were four drawings of a girl. She was faceless, an empty circle topped with fair hair in a bun. Written in pencil along the drawings was:

Anya, Act I.    Arrival.
Anya, Act I.    Nightdress.
Anya, Act II.   Ball Dress.
Anya, Act III.  Travelling clothes.

I felt a pang when I saw the ghost of the girl I was growing into and the clothes she was going to wear. A jacket edged with fur: a Russian cap and a muff; a high-necked nightdress massed with frills; an ankle-length ball dress.

'I'm doing you and Peachey,' Cliff said, sewing as he talked. 'I'm also doing Sir's dinner clothes, including a dreamy cape.' He went on sewing, viciously fast, at a long band of black velvet. He put it down unwillingly, climbed from the steps and came over to look at the sketches.

'Not bad, are they? That new woman is clever. But she's a bag of nerves. Have you noticed how all our designers are neurotic? But aren't we all, dear, aren't we all? Anya's a real little Russian aristocrat, isn't she? Look at that sable muff. She must look good when she first comes on, you know. She's been on the train all the way from Paris to that old house and its orchard. The trans-Siberian Railway took days, but Anya had Charlotta to look after her *and* that jumped-up valet; and they had a travelling samovar to make themselves fresh tea. Mustn't waste time. Where's my tape measure?'

He knelt at my feet, measuring from waist to floor.

'Peachey Pratt says you've been rehearsing

without a practice skirt,' he observed.

'I've been meaning — '

'I watched yesterday, dear,' said Cliff, putting the tape round my waist and pulling it in until I couldn't breathe. 'Hm, you can lose a bit before I do that braided jacket. As I was saying, when you make that entrance in Act I — well, you can't do it, can you? Running around in *tights*. Women moved differently in long skirts. They used to glide in those days, you know, dear. Maybe if they were young and happy they bounced. What they did not do was *slouch*.'

He scrabbled behind the table among a pile of fabric.

'Here you are, then.' He threw me a skirt. It was voluminous dark serge with bands of white braid round the hem and a waist fastened with gigantic hooks and eyes.

'Cliff! You're an angel.'

'Yes, I am. Put it on, take off those horrible tights, and see if you can be more like a real lady.'

The rehearsal had started when I slipped in. I was given a furious frown from Gareth because I was late, and an approving raise of eyebrows from Periandra when she saw the skirt.

We worked on into the evening. I thought the play was beginning to jell. What had Dad

181

said once? That it was like making a sauce. You took separate ingredients and they looked as if they could never be blended into a single thing. You stirred slowly and gently and had patience, and it happened.

There we were in the old gym: the actors of Dad's company, familiar faces and voices. We were playing the scene when the Ranevsky family arrived home in the middle of the night. My father's understudy was reading Gayev's lines, and the actress who played my half-sister Varya had a scene with him. I had finished my own scene with Varya and made my exit, trailing off to bed after my long journey across Russia so tired that I was asleep on my feet.

I did not watch before my next entrance, but sat thinking about Anya, and feeling about Anya. I was far away. Through the deafness of thought I heard the words before my cue: 'If only God would help us,' Varya said.

A voice replied. A soft voice. It was my father.

'Anya's standing in the doorway,' whispered Varya on cue.

'What!' He turned, and as I stood staring, he was utterly changed. The toughness was gone, the sardonic personality melted. The man standing there was gentle, self-mocking, weak. He was a Russian. He was Gayev.

I went forward, my arms out.

'I can't sleep. I just can't,' I said.

He came towards me, took my face between his hands and kissed me. 'My dear little girl! You're not just a niece to me, you're an angel. You're everything to me. Please believe me . . . ' he said, his voice broken, his face streaming with tears.

★ ★ ★

At the corner of the square under the trees, the Rolls was waiting. Dad and I walked over together.

'I had to keep moving; wasn't allowed to park; the police are being very dodgy to-night, Sir Robert,' said Harris, my father's chauffeur. He liked to prove that his job was achieved by great ingenuity and looked hopefully at Dad after he'd done this.

'Mm,' said my father, not listening. He expected miracles all the time, and if you pointed out that you'd performed them, never praised you. But Harris still looked surprised and disappointed.

On the drive home my father was abstracted, picking his front teeth with a fingernail and staring from the window. I was still. It was the first time Dad and I had acted, spoken lines to each other, since the New York play. I had remembered the intenseness of my father's presence on-stage: the feel of being near something bright and hot. But I'd forgotten, or I had never known, that if you began to get it right he threw the light and warmth towards you — a stream of brightness you could bathe in. When Gayev had looked at me and spoken the words of a weak man to a child he loved, it had happened. If I could learn to play right, this extraordinary feeling would come back again. If I could do it right . . .

Dad looked over at me and yawned.

'Hungry?' he said. 'I told Harriet we'd need liver and bacon, and plenty of it.'

Dad and I had supper together. He kissed me before I went to bed. 'Good night, Puss. Not bad.'

★ ★ ★

Ben telephoned me at 7.30 one morning just as I was coming down the stairs for breakfast, feeling frail. I picked up the receiver to stop its noise and Ben's lively voice had the effect of cold water, painful and refreshing:

'Got you! I feel like a butterfly-hunter. I've been after you for days with my net and now I've got you. How about supper to-night?

This hot weather isn't going to last and I want to take you to the country and see you in a different setting. What time do you break? Eight?'

'Might be later if we go on — '

'You won't, there's a lighting rehearsal. I checked. Going to have dinner with me?'

'Yes please.'

He said he would pick me up and not to worry if I was late, he was used to hanging about. 'I'll stand and think of you acting away in there and wish I could watch,' he said sentimentally.

It was a sizzling day, hot as Africa, and the heat worked on the actors, loosening and freeing them. They sweated and acted better.

I felt tired and pleased with myself as I changed out of my now-shabby practice skirt and put on a dress I'd brought with me to the theatre — blue and green chiffon, Greek again: Tam and I still liked the *Troilus* designs best. As I came down the corridor walking with a swing, I collided with Periandra. She was shuffling along in a faded dressing-gown that ought to have been called a 'wrapper.' She looked worn out and older than fifty, but her face revived with the liveliest curiosity when she looked at me.

'Going out to dine with Sir?'

I said vaguely no I wasn't going out with

Dad, it was nothing, just some food. My ruse was pathetic against Periandra, who threw her robe round her like a toga and said she must just ask Sir if there were any messages for her. Had she told me she was expecting a call from Jo Losey? She went ahead, her walk springing, and, as her instinct had correctly told her, she pushed open the doors and saw Ben.

'Ah, Sidney!' she said commandingly, looking, not at the indifferent Sidney in his cubby-hole, but straight at Ben leaning against the notice board under old first night greetings telegrams.

'Hallo, there,' said Ben, looking beyond Periandra and giving me an intimate smile.

When I went over to him he took my shoulders and kissed my cheek. Periandra looked satisfied and disapproving. She went off, for the moment quite forgetting Jo Losey.

Ben laughed a lot about her as we drove through the dusty evening. 'She looks like the company gossip to me.'

'Right.'

'Does it worry you?' His manner was proprietary and I found this amusing.

'No, I don't mind being discussed by Periandra,' I lied.

He drove out of London through strange

roads he seemed to know well. Soon we'd left the city and passed through orderly ugly suburbs and at last as it grew dark we were in country with elm trees and water meadows, the high grass not yet cut for hay and old houses with drives. 'I'm taking you to a favourite place of mine. The Running Waiter. You'll like it. It's got a bit of river and a garden. The food's okay in a kind of mini-steak way. Anyway I like it and I think you will. I must tell you, the last time I went there . . . '

He began a story of one of his adventures, a well-observed tale, with a ludicrous side. He laughed. So did I. We exchanged looks which were happy and full of sex.

The Running Waiter turned out to be a smart-alec pub full of commuters drinking gin. Ben took me through to the restaurant, where he'd booked a table, and during the meal we talked mostly about his work. I still didn't want to talk about mine, and Ben seemed pleased to chat and make me laugh. I found it rather touching and like him that he was stoutly loyal to his own paper. Had I read the articles he'd told me about? Did I know this new poet? Directly my play was on, I must come with him and see round his paper in its new building in the city. Did I remember that medical piece he was doing? It

187

was to be printed next week.

We had white wine for dinner and there were roses in a bowl on the table which smelled like those in the garden at home, tea-roses with a particularly sharp scent of their own. After the meal Ben leaned on his elbows and drew patterns on the cloth with a spoon. When he looked up, his blue eyes were hot.

'Let's go for a walk.'

I agreed without a word. He paid the bill and we threaded our way through the noisy crowds of people, down a stone passage and out into the close still night. Cars glittered under the lights of the pub car-park, and under the light of a circular moon swimming in a navy-blue sky.

He linked his arm round my waist, and walking as close as if we were tied together we went down a rutted country pathway with hedges on either side. The pub shrank into the distance, and the noise of music and voices grew faint. At last we were far enough to be able to hear a grasshopper and the ringing silence, faintly stirred by traffic a mile away.

'Here's a field,' Ben said. In silence, we climbed the gate. The waist-high buttercups had no colour in the moonlight except a sheen-like paleness, and they brushed against us as we picked our way through them.

We went across the field on to the other side, by a deep flower-starred ditch. Ben took off his jacket and we lay down on it. The jacket sprang upwards on the flowers and grasses until it was I who pressed it down with my weight, and Ben rolled on top of me and we began to kiss.

We stopped after a while and I looked upwards. I could see the sky behind his shiny blond head which gleamed, like a spirit's, in the dimness.

'Candida.'

'Mm.'

'You're very beautiful.'

'You are too.'

He didn't bother to smile.

We kissed again and it grew to more than kissing, and just when I thought 'Oh yes, yes,' he stopped. He was silent for far too long and then he said:

'Are you a virgin?'

I didn't answer.

'I must know.'

I put my arms round his neck but he did not bend down again. I couldn't see his face in the dark, only the shiny sky.

'Answer me, Candida.'

'I'm afraid the answer's yes.'

'Why afraid?'

'Because almost nobody is and I don't want to be.'

'So you thought it might as well be me.'

I could have been angry but I was no such thing because you can't be angry with a man when you are desperately attracted, lying on your back among five-foot-high buttercups and about to be kissed breathless. We started kissing again but that was strictly all.

We sang on the way home.

'Ben.'

'Yes?'

'Why are we happy when we didn't . . . '

'Don't be a nit, Candida,' he said, and kissed me as he drove, which was unsafe and very exciting.

It was late and still hot when we arrived home. I hoped for more kissing and was uncomfortable and longing. I wanted it settled. Were we going to or not? But Ben did not say and I found I couldn't. I contented myself by returning his kisses violently, and feeling rather flat because his own were more controlled than they'd been in the buttercups.

'Shall I see you again soon?'

'Very soon. Very soon.'

He put up his hand and outlined my face and when I looked at him I saw that in the gloom his eyes looked black.

I went into the house at last and closed the

door and leaned against it, listening to his steps receding, and to the sound of his car as he drove down the hill. It was very silent in the house and from the skylight two stories up a pale radiance fell, rather like moonlight. There was a smell of lilies from a tall vase of them on the stairs. The grandfather clock ticked loudly. I felt lonely and excited and my lips hurt.

As I went quietly up the stairs, I came to the first landing and saw a spear of light under my father's door. I smiled, thinking that he was awake and still at work. I went down the passage towards the flight of stairs that led to my room.

There was a glare of light.

'Candida!'

My father stood in the doorway, the light behind him as if he were in a religious picture, an effect exaggerated by the long, dark red robe he wore.

'Hallo, darl — ' I began, and he cut in:

'Where have *you* been?'

His tone was like a slap in the face.

I stood blinking at the brightness.

'Out,' I said.

'Don't be impertinent. Where have you been?'

'Out to dinner — why — what's happened?'

'Happened? What should have happened?' he repeated, in a gibing mimicry of my voice. 'Do you know that it is one o'clock in the morning and that we are due at rehearsal early? Do you consider' — he went on, folding his arms and looking at me savagely — 'that you are so talented, so professional, that you can do the part on your head? You, apparently, do not need to do any more work. That's nice. And who has been taking you tagging round London, making you look the colour of chalk? One of my actors?'

'Ben Nash — you met him the other night — he's Dr. Laurie's — '

'Spare me,' said my father, holding up his hand. 'Spare me the friend-of-the-Hippocratic-Oath bit. I know the man. Some fifth-rate journalist.'

He studied me. I just stood.

'Upstairs,' he said at last. 'And if you are one minute late for rehearsal, or don't play exactly the way I want, I'll sack you. I'll give the part to a cleverer actress than you'll ever be. She won't be difficult to find!'

★    ★    ★

Nerves woke me early, and I was bathed and dressed and in the kitchen drinking coffee long before the car had driven up to the door

192

to take Dad and me to the Royalty.

I had come into the kitchen hoping to find Harriet. When I saw her, the cloud was darker than ever round her. She gave me breakfast in silence and went into the scullery without a word. I followed her, carrying my mug.

Her back was turned and her head was bent, she was busy grinding coffee beans. A fragrant smell, and the grinder's thin scream, filled the scullery.

'Harriet.'

She didn't turn. I touched her and she started as if she'd been stabbed. She switched off the grinder and turned a haggard face towards me.

'I'm sorry. Did I startle you?'

'Yes.'

'Harriet, what's the matter?'

'Nothing. I have a headache.'

At once I was ashamed. I was a selfish bitch, wrapped up in my own affairs when all the time here was someone close to me who might be ill.

'What is it? Can I get the doctor? Do let me help.'

'Don't be silly, I am not so decrepit I can't get down the road to Dr. Laurie if I'm ill. You don't look so good yourself, while we're on the subject.'

'I didn't sleep well.'

'That's obvious. Why?'

'Dad caught me coming in late. It was ridiculous. Like a Pinero play. Did I know the time. That kind of thing. Harriet, he is absurd! Most girls of my age left home years ago. Someone'll have to tell him.'

'Sir isn't interested in your followers,' Harriet said pityingly. 'You said it yourself when Tam was on the tiles. He growls over your men but that's not what he's growling about. It's the fact that it won't help your work. Work. And by the colour of your face he isn't going to get much of that out of you to-day.'

'Shall I smooth him down?'

'You do just that,' said Harriet, switching on the grinder again and letting it scream its head off.

I was in the car before Dad, who came loping down the pathway like a boxer. He jumped in lightly, wearing gym shoes laced to the toe, still in the boxer's image. He looked crackling with energy.

The car moved off. He did not glance at me.

'Good morning, Dad,' I said to his profile. 'Am I still in the dog-house?'

'What repulsive English you use. You are not in a dog-house but in a Rolls. How's your talent this morning?'

'Dazzling.'

I guessed exactly the look of sardonic approval I would get for this impertinence.

* * *

We worked. We just worked. We rehearsed until the play was oiled and sweet-running and every delicate indication of character was right. We worked until voice and gesture and thought seemed to be one.

My father was a demanding director. I remembered it from the days of the Racine, but now I was more deeply involved, and had none of the innocent confidence of the beginner. He was patient and fierce, noisy and gentle, warm sometimes, and then bitterly sarcastic. Sometimes we felt exhausted and depressed, sometimes we felt sulky. We always felt alive.

Working on one's imagination was draining, and I found other things waned into unimportance. I wasn't interested in the way I looked, unless it was as Anya looked when I spoke in her voice. I wasn't interested in the newspapers or in messages from my friends or in the sunny sultry weather. I slept badly and Anya was in my dreams, like the doppel-gänger she had become. Sometimes I thought I'd walk into a room one day and see myself, as Anya, seated on a chair.

The only person I did think about was Ben. For moments during the long days and evenings of disciplined emotion, I thought of Ben in the buttercups, his hair shiny in the moonlight, his face, his sex. Yes, I thought about that and felt disturbed and melting.

Rehearsals broke at three in the morning of the day we were to open and when we'd arrived home in the damp, dew-sodden dawn, Dad said:

'Sleep till late, please.'

'I never will.'

'Svengali speaking!' he said, pinching my cheek for the first time in days.

Ringing with nerves I lay down and slept without a dream.

★ ★ ★

Late in the morning of the day of the first night, Tam came into my room with a breakfast tray.

'How do you feel?' she inquired, looking me over professionally.

'Like a rough Channel crossing and I wish you weren't dressed in that sailor suit. Ugh. I can't eat.'

'Don't you like my clothes? I thought the

Jack Tar effect rather fascinating. I'm glad you feel sick, darling. Dad says only half-wits have no nerves.'

'Don't quote the Oracle at me.'

'Why not? If you've any sense you'll go and sacrifice a few burnt offerings to it. I do regularly,' she said. 'Talking about victims, I saw your journalist. In a pub near the theatre. He sent fond love and said he keeps ringing but never gets you. I told him how it is before opening night.'

She peered at me and burst out laughing.

'You are a fool. Why are you so secretive? I know you fancy him madly, and what's the big mystery? I'm not secretive about old Johnnie B. He's back, and we've got to go to his exhibition next week, you and I, and give him a publicity boost. I've fixed it all up. So it's serious with you and the man with the hair, is it?'

'No.'

'Okay, okay, don't say anything, your face is shouting at the top of its voice. I quite *like* him, you know. He's rather dishy, and he likes me and that's good too. I'll see him at the party to-night, I expect. Have you got him a seat for the performance? How serious *is* it?'

'Tam — '

'Answer!' she said dramatically.

So of course I didn't.

' 'Bye, darling,' said Tam, leaning forward to hug me and only just managing not to spill boiling coffee all over the bed.

There was nothing to do but wait. Last night's dress rehearsal had gone middlingly well; certainly it had looked wonderful. There had been final instructions; criticisms of our costumes (mine for the Ball scene didn't fit); and an inevitable last-minute emergency because the actor who played the valet, a tough man called Mike, fell and thought he'd broken his ankle. It proved to be a sprain. Heavily bound up with Elastoplast, Mike said he could manage opening night. 'Actors love alibis against possible bad notices,' said Periandra heartlessly.

Everyone was morose and exhausted. Except Dad. He sent a message via Mrs. Brown for me to have a late lunch with him. It was a Royal Command; Mrs. Brown was using capital letters again.

When I arrived he was in the dining-room eating pepper-corned steak, his favourite meal. He continued for a moment to dictate a letter to Mrs. Brown with his mouth full. Then:

'Sit down, child. I've told Harriet to bring you a steak like mine.'

'But Dad, I only had breakfast a little while ago and you know I hate — '

'Peppercorns are good for liver and heart. Thighs and sinews too,' said Dad, who often spoke a kind of garbled Shakespeare. 'Peppercorns are also excellent for the nerves. Like curry, the heat is cooling.'

'I'm cool,' I said, sitting beside him.

My father cocked an eye at Mrs. Brown, busy with the inevitable papers heaped at the serving-table.

'Mrs. Brown! Do not scuffle! Are you a mouse? And what are you dishing up for me over there? Am I to be given some inferior film script for pudding?'

She gave a weak smile. To-day, in green leather, her hair straight and short (she'd given up curls last Wednesday when Dad made a joke about them), she looked smart. What was not smart was her expression: lovelorn; Dad-lorn.

'Off with you, Mrs. Brown. I wish to speak to my child,' said my father, pouring carrot juice into a Georgian wine glass.

When we were alone he glanced at me. How well I knew that penetrating look. An arrow shaft? A surgeon's knife?

'Well, Puss. So you're pleased with your performance.'

'Not at all.'

'Good. Never be satisfied with your art or it'll go rotten. You are quite good. Quite. But minuscule. The picture's too small. You must take risks, be more daring. The clothes you wear on stage are made to be looked at hundreds of feet away. Emotions, too. Use bold controlled strokes.'

I listened like a person on a strange road already certain I would forget the turnings to left and right, knowing I desperately needed every one of them.

'Tell you something else,' said Dad, crunching peppercorns. 'You are holding back.'

'Of course I'm not.'

'Don't contradict Me,' he said. Then, softly, his voice vibrating, 'You're holding back a part of yourself. You're cheating.'

'I don't understand.'

'Oh yes you do. A performance must be all. An actor must give the lot. The mind must never stray, there must be no reservations, or it shows.'

I swallowed.

'Off with you now. That's all I want to say. Ah, here's Harriet with your peppered steak. Put it on a tray and take it up to her bedroom, Harry! When she's eaten it, pull the curtains and see that she goes back to sleep. Steak and sleep, Candida. We'll make an actress of you yet.'

Once again I swore I couldn't sleep a wink.

And slept at once. Harriet woke me at five o'clock. I opened my eyes, smiled at her, remembered it was opening night and felt violently sick.

She said, reading my look, 'I've run a bath. Come along. There's a time to live and a time to die!'

During the bath I kept my mind off the play and on Ben. Ben! He'd be there to-night and we'd talk and kiss. The relief, the joy and relief, of being with Ben when the ordeal was over!

I wrapped myself in the old Roman bath-robe and trailed into the bedroom. I was sitting at the dressing-table brushing my hair and keeping my mind a careful blank when there was a knock and Ventura came in. Her Italian saint's face was all smiles. She looked as if she were in one of those stained glass windows where the heavens opened and well-built angels came flying down. She beamed, muttered something that sounded like 'good fortune, good fortune,' gave me a letter and went out.

I picked up the letter, and saw it was from Ben. I scarcely knew his writing, but it had his paper's title on the envelope. I looked at the writing with a little spasm of the heart, thinking it was like him to write and wish me luck just the moment I needed it, and how I wanted so much, so much, to see him. I tore open the envelope.

'Candida love. I'm so sorry but I can't make the play to-night after all. I've been sent off on a job to Wales which will take days. I know how busy you are going to be, and as the Welsh thing is pretty complicated, perhaps it won't be possible to be in touch. I send you all my warm wishes for to-night and the future. I know you'll be famous and happy.

'Ben.'

I read it twice. At first I didn't believe what the letter said, and then I had to, because it was perfectly clear. Ben had thought it over and decided on a nice clean cut. An emergency operation to save the patient. Which patient? Me or him? But Ben knew that I was half in love with him, and wanted to be loved by him, he'd seen it as we lay together and it was he who'd said no. He had told me, when I telephoned, that he was coming to the play to-night but that must have been to shut me up. He had wanted to tell me, in a letter because it was cool, that I was thrown over.

I stared at the letter. He'd always been such a lively man. But one who belonged to himself. He had been attracted to me, drawn to me, I had thought I touched him. But he didn't want to love me and he'd done the fair thing.

I didn't cry. I just felt dreary and rather ill. I thought of the play with longing and relief. I dressed and ran down the stairs. The car was waiting, Harris sitting in the front staring into vacancy. I climbed in and shortly afterwards Dad came swinging down the path and into the car. We moved off.

Dad said: 'No talking on the way to the theatre.'

'Why not?'

He took no notice of my gloomy manner but merely replied: 'Silence is best.'

We got down at the stage door: Dad to disappear to his star dressing-room (large as a drawing-room), me up two floors to the dressing-room I shared with Periandra.

She was already fully dressed in her costume as Charlotta, her face chalk-white, her eyes enormous, false eyelashes and purple marks enhancing them. She was drinking champagne.

'I told Tamara not to come round before the performance. You need peace,' she said.

She sipped her champagne and sat watching as I stripped off my clothes, pulled on a cotton gown and a broad elastic ribbon to keep my hair away from my face, and began to paint my eyes.

'What is wrong, Candida?'

'Nothing.'

'Nerves?'

'That's right.'

'Nerves are essential,' said Periandra calmly. 'No, darling, use this — ' offering me a particular eye-pencil which she never allowed anyone to touch.

At last the stage manager's voice, 'Curtain up on Act One,' came over the intercom loudspeaker that was fixed in all our dressing-rooms. The performance had started. Through the loudspeaker we could hear the actors speaking the lines we knew as well as our own names. Periandra and I sat in silence. The room was hot.

It came to Charlotta's cue, and Periandra, cool as if she were going shopping in Regent Street, stood up, pulled her corsets straight under her striped dress and went out. I heard her voice over the loudspeaker.

A few minutes later it was my cue. I walked out of the dressing-room and down the stairs into the wings. For a moment I remembered Ben wasn't out front, and was my wounded bruised self. And then . . . there was the shadowed room, the old nursery in Holy Russia; and it was my old nursery too, full of hope and youth and sadness. And there, across the room by the bookcase, was — not my father — but my dear Uncle Gayev with his sweet bearded face.

I went into the luminous space that was both the stage and another life and I saw Gayev stare at me. The radiance that belonged to him bathed me, and tears came brimming into my eyes and my voice as I ran towards him.

# 8

Impossible to sleep. When the end of the party finally came it was almost daylight, and in our dim garden the lavender was starting to put on its colour again. I went slowly to bed, to lie awake, watching the sky between the undrawn curtains.

Last night the first performance of *The Cherry Orchard* had gone wonderfully. Or rather, we believed it had. How could we say? All actors from Dad to beginners like me knew that you could not always claim success because of a roar of applause, the warmth sweeping from audience to players. Often Dad's company had been full of excited hope after the first night and woken next day to read that the play, production, actors, or all these, had far from pleased the critics.

I had no idea about my own performance either. Onstage Dad had kissed me, pressing me in his arms. That had been for the audience. But when we had said good night to each other at the long end of the long party his expression had been enigmatic. Practised at translating my father's changing face, I couldn't read it this time.

During the party I had been with crowds of fellow actors or close to my father. He called me over time and again and stood with a heavy arm round my shoulders while he talked. First I had played Anya, and then I'd acted a joyful Candida for the rest of the night. Now I was too tired to sleep.

The bedroom door opened and Tam came in. Her arms were full of newspapers.

'Oh God!'

'I know, I know. I fixed to get them early. Calm down! I haven't even *opened* them. It isn't fair to read someone's notices before they do.'

She plumped on the bed and spread the papers in front of us. We looked at them without moving. Tam said at last: 'Here goes.'

We each picked up a newspaper. Years of reading theatre notices had taught us exactly which page to look for, how to fold the paper expertly so that the notice stared upwards.

In five minutes we knew the answer. The critics were unanimous: the play was a success.

So was I.

'Candida Waring, a dazzling new arrival . . .'

'In the part of Anya, this touching new actress . . .'

'Robert Waring's daughter, a stunning . . .'

'This remarkable production also gives us a brilliant performance of Anya by . . .'

Many of the notices carried large pictures of my father with the actress who played Madame Ranevska. Two or three of them showed Anya too. I looked at my pictured face close to my father's. I read the notices again.

Tam read aloud:

'There is, in her performance, the recognisable Waring touch, delicate and strong.' She threw down the paper and bent forward to give me a hug which nearly choked me.

'You've done it! You've done it! Oh darling, I'm so happy for you! And so jealous!'

The whole of theatre people's philosophy was in my sister's laughing voice.

We went down to the kitchen, creeping past my father's bedroom, the floor-boards creaking. Harriet was making coffee. Wearing a white overall like a chemist's, every grey hair brushed, she looked as composed as somebody who'd just had twelve hours sleep. She had had two. When she saw us she slammed down the coffee pot and seized the newspapers. She read them sitting on the kitchen table. At last she said: 'And this is the girl who told us if she trod on a stage again she'd be sick.'

'I nearly was.'

'Candy and her stomach. She's always feeling sick. At great moments of one's life, one should have a sound digestion,' said Tam. Her face was very white and her freckles stood out.

Harriet looked at her. 'How's my baby taking it?' she asked.

Tam answered innocently: 'I've got it all worked out. Candy's success will be *useful*. It will make much more of a story later when they start raving about Me.'

I did not imagine the capital letter. It was the first time I'd heard her use it.

Harriet had breakfast with us that morning, a thing she hadn't done for a long time. Common joy joined us as it had done the day Dad won his Hollywood Oscar, and another day when he'd gone to the Palace to be knighted and we three had waited in the courtyard outside.

Tam and I went back upstairs to have baths and dress. She went on talking. I was glad to listen to the stream of shop, jokes, gossip about how my career (not forgetting her own) could be altered by this morning's news. Every now and then I thought of Ben and pushed him away.

The rest of the house was quiet. Its hush was not allowed to break after first nights until half past ten, a law older than we were.

Whether the notices were warm or cold, full of praise or to our eyes cruel and derisory, his own newspapers lay unread in the hall until the grandfather clock struck the half-hour. Then Harriet carried them into my father's room on his breakfast tray.

I was fidgeting around in the nursery when she looked in. '*He* wants you.'

The sun was flooding through the skylight as the spots had flooded over us in the play. I knocked. I heard the imperious: 'Come.'

He was propped in the double bed that he and my mother had shared, a great barge of polished wood, dark as treacle, which legend said had belonged to Napoleon. Tam once remarked that megalomania had set in when Dad bought that bed.

The room, like everything else belonging to him — house, bed, car — was far too big. Trophies filled it. Paintings, photographs, shelves littered with Russian lacquer boxes, a silver loving-cup, a glass-topped table displaying medals, plaques and orders, the 'Freedom of Cities' that Dad would never visit again.

He looked at me as he had done when we said good night. I had no idea what he was thinking.

'Come here.'

I went over to take the muscular hand

stretched towards me. I sat on the edge of the bed.

'Well? Aren't you going to thank me?'

'Oh Dad — I — '

'Oh Dad I'm now a star, and oh Dad I shall want better billing and more money and I dare say, oh Dad, I shall be off to make a motion picture and shan't be at your Royalty much from now on.'

'Oh, Dad, you are a fool!'

We laughed and kissed.

'It has worked,' he said with satisfaction. 'They can see what I see. It's always been in you.'

'I didn't know.'

'Why should you?' he said impatiently. 'It's a pity an actor ever discovers why people want him, why, instead of other actors, he is the one they queue for, the one they have that affair-in-the-mind with. *I'm* not going to tell you. I didn't know about myself for years. Once you find out, you'll overplay it. The critics this morning say you're 'radiant.' Don't start *being* radiant. That would be a disaster. It is exciting when they like you but you'll have to learn to live with it and it's hard. You'll also have to learn not to listen to them. Throw away the notices. Forget the praise. Stop your ears, like Ulysses, from the treatment they're going to give you — starting now!'

The telephone began to ring.

⋆   ⋆   ⋆

I was given the treatment. The telephone rang all day, there were photographers, TV programme producers, newspapermen. Foreign journalists also visited us, and Dad, Tam and I (not forgetting Sheba sentimentally posed by Dad's feet) were photographed over and over again, in determined family groups. Dad would always make us laugh just when the photographer wanted us all tender. Two film companies asked if I would do tests, a clothes designer wrote to say he was creating a range of 'Candida' clothes. What made Dad laugh most was a cable from Hollywood offering me the part of Princess Elrigg in a Viking epic.

'Who are they kidding?' shouted Dad, waving the cable.

'Why?' asked Tam, determinedly bright nowadays. 'Everyone loves epics and you've made three.'

'Aha. But I've seen the script and they have omitted to mention that Princess Whatshername has her tongue cut out half-way through,' said Dad.

There was never an hour when I wasn't

busy during the day, or in the evenings either, because for two weeks we played *The Orchard* solid without bringing in the Ghilain farce. It was the time that I completely forgot Ben and was happy.

My father took over my life. He would not allow me to answer the telephone or make decisions, set Mrs. Brown as watchdog, and dictated detail by detail what I should do, as if I were mad or six years old.

'When that Swedish journalist comes, the first thing to say to him is . . . ' etc., etc.

'What dress are you wearing? No. Trousers and that blue sweater is better.'

'Mrs. Brown! While I'm out see that My child carries out My instructions to the letter!'

In a softened moment after we'd had a heated argument about my attending a charity premiere ('I am not interested in your charitable inclinations but in seeing you in the gymnasium') he did say kindly: 'It is important at present, Puss, for us to think everything out.'

In the middle of a particularly complex day of his own work and after an hour of being that old bore Svengali to me, he commanded us to luncheon.

'Prisoners in the Château d'If got more to eat!' complained Tam. 'I want another apple.'

'Fifteen calories each. Famous or fat, which is it to be?' asked Dad. 'Mrs. Brown! Put the apples out of reach. I have news, girls. I do not wish you to travel by bus any more.'

We looked at him in surprise.

'Don't think this means you can have your own cars,' he added. 'But Candida's success . . . and your own modest efforts, Tamara, make it impossible for me to give you girls the common touch any more, much as I regret it. I gather, Candida, that you were asked for your autograph three times yesterday on a Number 271A.'

'How did you know that?' asked Tam. 'I bet Candy never told you.'

'I know Everything,' said my father simply. 'There is nothing wrong with you giving autographs at the stage door, but if you continue to take buses, you will lose a certain mystery we wish to preserve.' He looked me over, his head on one side, a conjurer with a rabbit or a dove. From that day, Tam and I were shuttled to and fro from the Royalty in Dad's car. It had been more relaxing to hop on a bus.

The days were too crowded for me to have time to be miserable over losing Ben. What had time to do with it? You don't 'lose' people at all, they hang about in your mind, boring and hurting you by being there when their physical selves are not. I could pretend it didn't hurt, but sooner or later I'd wallow in it and then it was worse. I re-read the letter, now squashed and dirty from lying in my handbag. I thought about the way he looked and the tone of his voice. I remembered the way we'd kissed.

I often wondered why I missed him so much, why I'd become so fond of him, why he'd attracted me. I wanted to find out so that I could cure it, taking an antidote to a love philtre. It couldn't be that he was merely attractive: I lived in a world where everybody was. Many actors were actually beautiful, all had strong personalities. Ben belonged somewhere out of our atmosphere of emotion, roars of laughter, tears we could summon when we wanted them. He had a cheerful freedom from the uneasy imagination. Although he was a writer, he seemed to me to epitomise the open air, away from an enclosed world of feeling. I had been tremblingly attracted to him: even when we touched by accident. I missed this mysterious pleasure. My world was flattened now he wasn't in it.

One morning when I was being fitted for a new dress that my friend Cliff had kindly designed and made for me, my sister came bursting into the room. She was full of her mid-morning energy and when she saw me stopped in mid-bound as if putting on invisible brakes.

Cliff, on his knees pinning my hem, didn't bother to turn round.

'I'll wager that is Tamara. Don't thunder like that, dear, you make the floor shake.'

She moved into his view.

'Those colours are too strong for you. You look like one of those nasty ices, Wopper or Big Time or whatever they call themselves, raspberry outside and strawberry in the middle. Always ask me before you venture into pink and red.'

'Don't be catty, Cliff,' said Tam. 'I look fascinating. Candy may be the big thing at present but you'd better get it into that head of yours that *I'm* next. Dad's promised I can play in Shakespeare in the winter. That sexy Audrey in *As You*. So just look out!'

'You don't do so badly in the Ghilain. Your performance is coming on. And what's this I hear about the serial on telly?' retorted Cliff, always more up-to-date with the company's news than they were.

'I haven't signed the contract yet — '

'Don't be coy. I met the TV director at a party last night — a *very* tiresome man, but mad about you.'

Cliff had successfully silenced Tam, who

216

now wore the actress's expression, half delight, half superstition, when she hears exactly what she is hoping.

He had a few seconds of peace to go on with his fitting while Tam helped herself liberally to my scent.

'I really came in to tell you that Johnnie B's art show opens to-day,' she said, peering at her face in the glass. 'You and I have promised to go to the private view. Johnnie's laid on the Press. Can you wear that white dress you've got on? It'll be a good foil to mine.'

'Of course she can't, it won't be ready till the morning,' said Cliff witheringly. 'Candida, don't stand on one leg, dear, unless you want me to make a dress for a stork. And I do wish you'd cheer up. My little masterpieces have to be worn with a bit of sparkle. Why the long face? You're supposed to fizz.'

'She doesn't like you sticking pins in her,' said Tam. 'Hurry up. I want to tell her about my sex life and I'm not doing it with your big ears around.'

Cliff collected the pins from the floor, undid the dress and promised it would be ready in the morning. He kissed us good-bye impartially.

I sat on the bed. Tam sat beside me. She said coaxingly: 'You don't mind being at the private view, do you? Poor Johnnie needs some luck and he's excited at finding a place to hang the pix. He says he won't get the Press there unless we are.'

She peered at me. 'It's Ben, isn't it?' she said.

'How did you know?'

'I've known for days. It shows. Where's he gone? What happened? Did you go to bed — '

'No, we didn't. Perhaps that's why.'

When I began to talk about him it made it better and worse. It was a relief to tell her the miserable little story, but when you actually say out loud that your affair is over, your voice is like the written word, much, much stronger and more fatal than thought. I took the letter from my handbag and gave it to her.

She read it and grimaced.

'Not a thing you can do about that. It really is the push. Isn't it funny, the way men get away?'

I sat there sniffing and Tam patted me, speaking the words we all use to people who are sad, a litany for the suffering.

'There there, poor darling, I know just how you feel,' and 'Cheer up, what about a smile?' as if I were a child who'd banged his head. And the inevitable 'All you need is time. You'll see. It'll be better in time.' Those who comfort you for the loss of love always hold

218

an hour-glass in their hands.

She finally relinquished her role of comforter to the bereaved, visibly cheered up and started vivaciously to discuss which clothes we would wear to Johnnie Buckingham's private view. Tam always liked to talk about our clothes when we went around together; she wanted to achieve a double effect. The impact of Robert Waring's *two* actress daughters, she always said, must be *planned*.

'I thought I'd wear the new bright green one and you could be in that purplish pink that you wore at that lunch the other day. Then we'll be a sort of Matisse duet.'

When I was dressed, Tam was waiting impatiently in the hall. She dragged me over to a full-length mirror by the dining-room door to study both our reflections together. She appeared satisfied. There were long mirrors all over our house, hung on the same principle as the mirrors in the wings of the theatre, strategically placed so that we could see how we looked before entering a room.

'You look fine,' said Tam, generous because I was doing something for her, 'you're getting a bit hungry-looking. Losing weight too fast. I shall tell Dad.'

'You dare.'

'Afraid he'll guess about Ben, I suppose.

Relax. With both plays packing he's taken the eye off us. Johnnie and I went to an old movie at the Classic Theatre the other night, it was a nineteen-fifty science fiction one. I just love those, don't you? It's fun being frightened out of your wits. Where was I?'

'I can't think.'

'Oh, I know, it was this man from Mars with eyes that shot a sort of ray, yards long, which set things on fire. One burst with the ray and it was all hands to the pumps. Exactly like Dad! Well, darling, *his* ray is *definitely* switched off at present, because he saw me with Johnnie in the Green Room and he actually said Hallo. Johnnie went puce. I think he secretly admires Dad and is a celebrity snob.'

'Who isn't?'

'Don't be beastly, darling,' said Tam, who enjoyed being called names.

I was silent, thinking about Dad's all-seeing eye. 'I don't feel very confident,' I said at last. 'You never know when the ray's going to switch on again.'

Tam agreed that it would start working overtime if he knew I was hankering for Ben. She mimicked my father. 'Do you mean to tell me that this *hack* matters, compared with your work for Me?' She shuddered delightedly.

220

We took a taxi and as it crawled through the traffic into Mayfair I thought how I hated missing Ben, lacking Ben, wanting to share my success with Ben. It was like being ill just at the moment I wanted most to be healthy. The one relief was that my father didn't know. I couldn't bear his derisive tongue. I wasn't as strong as usual, and because of this had lost my power over Dad. It also occurred to me that he could actually be hurt too. He'd always prided himself that he understood us completely and could read our hearts. He would do this like a conjurer still enchanted at his own skill. Now I was glad that for once his omniscience wasn't working.

The taxi set us down at the corner of Curzon Street near a poky antique shop into which Tam barged, pushing the door and setting a Victorian bell jangling. A middle-aged woman seated at a desk loaded with glass paper-weights greeted us.

'Hi, Mrs. Aire. Any press yet?' asked Tam professionally. 'This is my sister Candida. Mrs. Aire, who's angelically letting us use her store-room.'

Before the lady and I had had time to shake hands Tam had hurried me on. It didn't matter, for Mrs. Aire was clearly a newly-recruited slave. Tam was getting more like my father every day. She had waved at Mrs. Aire with exactly his manner, perfectly certain of love and admiration. I followed her down a flight of stone steps into a damp-smelling cellar lit by bare bulbs strung round on flexes. The effect was macabre and curiously festive: a vampire's Christmas decorations.

Standing in the centre of the room, matching the horror-comic effect, was Johnnie Buckingham. He was dressed from head to foot in black, the medal gleamed on his chest, his hair was on end and an expression of despair on his face. A boy called Lewis whom we'd met once or twice before was pinning unframed paintings and drawings on peeling walls.

'No one's going to come. I've always had a sixth sense, it's being Slav. I know they won't come, I know it here,' said Johnnie, thumping the medal. Lewis ignored him and pinned up more drawings.

'I feel suicidal,' Johnnie said, catching sight of Tam and me. 'Hallo. Good of you to come. But why bother?'

'I told you I'd bring Candy and here she is,' said Tam. 'Say hallo nicely.'

'Thanks,' said Johnnie, taking my hand and gripping it sorrowfully.

Tam said: 'Johnnie's overcome with your notices and all the fuss they're making about you. He's seen *The Orchard* three times because of you. He's only seen the Ghilain twice, I may add.'

'You're great. Great,' Johnnie said, looking at me solemnly.

Earlier to-day my father had asked: 'How are you taking it when they tell you they like you? Feel a bit humble, eh, Puss?'

'Yes. Yes I do.'

'It'll wear off. Pity how that feeling goes,' throwing his eyes to the ceiling.

My sister, pitching her handbag into a corner, clambered up a step-ladder, attended by Lewis, whose slavish expression was similar to that of Mrs. Aire's. 'Lew. We've only got five minutes and I'm going to rehang these, they don't work. Where's the one you did with stamps and sealing-wax? And look, pass me that terrific one Johnnie did with the oven-cleaner. I *love* it. And where's the cat study? We can't sky it like that!'

She unhooked a large scarlet and white painting and passed it to Lewis, asking how much it was marked at.

'Ten,' muttered Lewis.

'Rubbish. Make it twenty.'

Tam championed those whom she believed ill-starred. Her conversations were always sympathetically spirited about the malignant fates that stopped people getting what they wanted and deserved. She liked bad news, so that she could start hacking at it to make it good.

I looked curiously round at the paintings and drawings. The work was haphazard, some of it clever and some false, none of it professional. It reminded me of the canvases and sketches that art students drag from bulging folders for their examinations. They groan beforehand that they've been commanded to produce at least fifty pieces of works, where are they going to find so much except in an old bottom drawer? A boy who sat next to me at art school had once done a dozen paintings the night before his exam, taking five minutes for each of them while watching television.

Lewis and Tam began to argue. My sister waved her arms passionately. Standing on the ladder, her stylish dress ignored, her moonstones jangling, she was as happy as a housewife doing the spring cleaning.

Johnnie came over to me. 'It was great of you to come. I hoped the Press might turn up for the show and then they could talk to you. Now I'm sure there won't be any Press and I feel a heel asking you.'

'I didn't come to see the journalists, I came to see the pictures!' I said. 'Which is yours?'

'The one Tam's rehanging. It's my best. It's called Hot Sun Strike Twelve, and I got the red with ketchup only it's gone a bit off . . . But it's a good red.'

Two men came down the cellar steps. Both had sharp unselfconscious faces and restless eyes. They reminded me of Ben, and looked round with the same curiosity. Johnnie shed his gloom like magic and hurried over, knowing instinctively that they were journalists. Tam joined them, bringing drinks.

Soon the men came over to me, Johnnie introduced us and a photographic session began. Nobody was more obliging to photographers than Tam. She would stand on her head if it made a good picture. She licked her lips to make them shine before every shot.

'What about over there with us both looking at that picture by the door. My sister could have her hand on it as if she's just bought it,' she said, pointing to 'Hot Sun Strike Twelve.' 'You're going to buy it, aren't you, darling?'

She wound her arm round my waist and we stood like the little princes in the tower.

The cellar began to fill with friends, other journalists, members of the Royalty company. Tam told one of the reporters that I had been to art school and was 'deeply interested in painting.' Her manner with newspaper people was over-eager, I thought.

225

Johnnie Buckingham bustled around, silver chain swinging, serving glasses of red wine which he called 'a little rough' and which made most of us choke. Flash bulbs popped like fireworks, people laughed, pictures were unpinned off the walls. Lewis went in search of a cash box. The party was going well and I decided that I could leave now.

'The overnight star. Well, well, what about a few kind words to yours truly?' said a voice suddenly.

It was the man I had seen in Harriet's kitchen. I remembered the closed sallow face, figure like a retired boxer's and maty manner.

'Jack Swift,' he said. 'Remember me? You've been doing a bit of good for yourself since we last met, to judge by the mighty roar of the Press.'

I didn't bother to answer and he didn't mind.

'I'm doing a feature for one of the old rags I work for,' he said. 'Give me a quote. Load of old rubbish, this show. What's the angle?'

'I don't know what you mean.'

'Quite simple. Something must be cooking. I'd like to know what. Tam going to marry that queer with the necklace? Wants to get him launched, does she? I think she'll find he isn't much good at this job. Doesn't know anything about painting if I'm any judge of it.'

He laughed heartily. I walked away and he followed me.

'Now, now, don't be uppity,' he said, not quite jokingly enough. 'You've only got one toe on the ladder, you know. Can't afford to make enemies of the Press just yet, even if your Dad does.' He put his hand on my arm. I gave a shove to try to shake it off.

'Now, now, ought to be nice, you know. Don't say you haven't been warned!' he said.

A photographer, standing nearby, joined us rather quickly. 'Old Jack getting out of hand?' he said, 'Just let us know and we'll remove him. He's inclined to be a nuisance when he's stoned. Won't be the first time we've wheeled him away.'

'Who the hell do you think — ' began Jack Swift angrily to the photographer. I was glad to escape.

It was a *Cherry Orchard* night. I walked through Berkeley Square and the busy Mayfair streets in the evening sun, cooling my temper. There was something menacing about Jack Swift. He made me angry. He also made me uneasy. A goose went over my grave.

'I'll ask Ben,' I thought. But I couldn't ask Ben anything any more.

★  ★  ★

The performance that night went better than ever, and at the end the audience cheered. When my father and I were driving home I turned to say something about the reception, still excited by it.

I looked at him, and I noticed his face was drawn, and that there were black smudges under his eyes. The signs of exhaustion gave me a painful feeling in my chest. It was the first time I'd looked at him, really looked at him, for days. Of course I acted with him at night, but that was different, for the man moving across the stage wasn't Dad, but his genius, his other, greater self. During the day, when he was my father, I had lately felt he was there to turn to about *my* prospects, *my* work, *my* future.

'Dad.'

'Yes, Puss?'

'Are you okay?'

'What do you mean, okay?' he replied, with his instantaneous edge at any suggestion of ill-health or fatigue.

'I just wondered.'

'I was working on the film script until late last night,' he said, frowning.

'You ought to go to bed early to-night.'

'Look after yourself, my girl, and leave me to decide at what hour I retire. Your sister Tamara is quite right about you.'

'What does that mean?'

'That you are a tiresome rusher-in with the first-aid box,' he said tartly.

He went straight upstairs when we arrived home, and sent for his dinner to be served in his room. I walked into the dining-room, where Harriet had left me a stately meal. It was useless to ask her to join me. And there was no sign of Tam, probably still wooing journalists. I sat down to eat.

There was no necessity for me to be alone. Actors are sociable creatures who enjoy getting together to talk and argue and tell funny stories. I could have someone with me at any time. But at present I felt cut off from my fellow players, both by my sudden success and by the fact that Dad kept me so much beside him. The actors were genuinely pleased for me. But envious too. They treated me with reserve.

I suppose also I was alone because the only man I really wanted to be with was Ben, and this feeling of mine sent out its own rays to other people.

Tam had remarked on this.

'Don't think people don't know when you're hankering. Fancying someone is like

229

having a certain kind of smell that puts others off.'

'How disgusting.'

'Isn't it? But apt.'

I sat ploughing through my supper, which was beautifully cooked as Harriet's food always was. I ate from loyalty; I had no appetite.

I went to bed, and lay in the dark, thinking about Ben. I wasn't in love, was I? How was I to know? I just knew that I liked him, wanted to be with him, was attracted to him, was light-hearted when he was there, quite light-headed in fact, and that he'd made me feel more fascinating, prettier, and wanted. I was an ungrateful bitch to hanker for a man when I had that great rich present of success. But I still remembered how it had felt lying in the buttercups, his heart pounding against me as if it were in my own chest.

I woke suddenly. Moonlight came through a gap in the curtains. I switched on my bedside light: quarter past two. And then I heard the noise that must have woken me. It was a groan.

I sprang out of bed and ran out of my room. Tam's bedroom door was still wide open — she evidently wasn't yet home — and as I ran along the landing I saw a light from the first floor.

My father's door was ajar. There was another gasping groan.

'Dad!'

He was lying against the pillows, his face drawn and yellowish. When he saw me he said with an effort:

'Puss. Sorry I woke you.'

'Darling! What's happened?'

'I don't know,' he said, speaking slowly. 'I've been very sick. And I have a pain across here.'

I was so frightened I nearly fainted. A chill ran over me. I spoke as calmly as I could:

'Let me get you comfortable.'

'No. I would rather not move.'

'I'll get some water.'

I went out of the room, not daring to run, which would show that I was frightened. I went down to the hall telephone and dialled.

'Doctor? It's Candida. My father's ill.'

'Candida? It's Ben,' said the voice sharply. 'What's happened?'

'Ben. Get the doctor quickly.'

'He's out on a night call. He left a number in case anyone called. What's happened?'

I gabbled my father's symptoms.

'I'll find Chris right away. Don't do anything. Just stay with him and I'll get him to you. 'Bye.'

My legs were shaking as I went back up the

stairs. I couldn't think that I'd just spoken to Ben again. I thought of nothing but my father.

When I came into the room he opened his eyes.

'The doctor will be here soon,' I said quietly.

He put out his hand. When I took it, it was damp with sweat. I sat beside him, holding his hand tenderly.

'How are you?'

'The pain's worn off a bit,' he said, with a shade of a smile.

He closed his eyes again. I sat and watched him. Love and anxiety filled me as I stared at the face which looked as if it had come from Olympus, the broad forehead with barred lines drawn by years of imperious frowns and riotous laughter, the sweaty curls streaked with grey. My father's face had always been so bony; he was proud of that, it was one of the reasons for his beauty. To-night the bones stuck out, the hollow cheeks were lakes of shadow.

I think I prayed.

My father moved, groaned a little, and was quiet again. And then I heard the sound I was waiting for — the frontdoor bell. Gently releasing his hand, I went out of the room, ran down the stairs and wrenched open the door. Dr. Laurie was standing in the misty dark. Behind him was Ben. The doctor came in first, carrying his bag.

'Hallo, my child, what's all this I hear? How's your father?' He was calm, confident, elderly. His age was a kind of blessing just then.

'He's the same, Doctor.'

'Any more sickness?'

'Not since I rang.'

'And you haven't moved him, of course?'

I shook my head.

'Good girl, you always had a sensible head on your shoulders,' he said. 'Ben will keep you company while I go up and have a look at the patient. Don't worry.'

He went up the stairs towards the square of light that came through my father's door.

I sat down on a wooden bench by the door. Ben lit a cigarette and said nothing. I hunched up in my dressing-gown, feeling cold. Looking down I noticed with surprise that I was barefoot. Ben continued to say nothing, but he watched the stairs.

The grandfather clock whirred and struck the hour.

As I sat there, shivering slightly, there was a kaleidoscope of pictures in my head: Dad's brilliant face under a curling eighteenth-century wig, Dad pouring carrot juice into a wine glass, Dad pinching Tam's cheek, Dad as Gayev, coming towards me, his eyes full of tears.

The door on the landing opened at last and Dr. Laurie came out. Ben and I hurried towards the stairs. The doctor moved quite slowly: his leisurely pace surprised me.

'It's all right, Candida, quite all right,' he said. 'He isn't very ill. You had a fine old fright, didn't you? Now, now, my child, I hope you aren't going to faint!'

I collapsed on to the bottom stair. Both men leaned over and pulled me up as if I were a child who'd tripped over. I stood between them shivering.

'What is it? What's wrong with him?' I said.

'He's got a perfectly commonplace but rather nasty virus which produces vomiting and stomach-ache. No rigidity. A fever. I thought it would be this when Ben told me about your telephone call, but I had to be sure. I've seen thirty similar cases this week. He'll be over it in forty-eight hours.'

'So he's all right . . .'

'Perfectly all right,' said Dr. Laurie, looking at his watch. 'I'll come in and see him to-morrow. You needn't worry about him for the rest of the night. I've given him an injection. He's already asleep. And the sickness has stopped. It's an odd bug, we haven't christened it yet. Well, well, my child, what you need is a cup of tea. Ben, support the lady to the kitchen and make her one. I shall have to get back to my other patient. A baby who can't make up his mind whether to be born to-day or to-morrow. Can I leave you both?'

The doctor eyed me, his calm droll self. 'You see Ben insisted on coming with me. Wants to study the work on location, he tells me. Let's see how he does with you as the patient. Off you go. Tea and a piece of thin toast.'

Ben and I went rather self-consciously down the hall towards the kitchen. I heard the front door close. And then, quite suddenly, I started to cry. It was too stupid. It was partly relief now that I wasn't afraid any more and it was partly because Ben was here. While I'd been so scared, I hadn't thought of anything but Dad. But now, the fact that Ben was with me and that I'd lost him seemed horribly sad. I choked and sniffed. It was ridiculous. Ben put his arm through mine and made comforting noises; he probably thought he was coping with a hysterical daughter suffering from shock. Maybe he was. He half led, half supported me to the kitchen, where Sheba woke up and wagged her tail at us. Ben planted me in a kitchen chair and went over to plug in the electric kettle.

'You've put too much water in it,' I said.

He took no notice but switched on the kettle and came over to sit beside me. I stopped crying but began to give those convulsive gasps that children do when they've had a crying bout.

'I'm sorry,' I said, after a shuddering choke.

'You've behaved extremely well.'

'Going on like a fool . . . ' Another gasp.

'Nothing of the kind. You telephoned for a doctor. You kept calm. And your father's okay. What's wrong with that?'

The kettle boiled and I was glad to get up and make us both a mug of instant coffee.

Up until now I had pretty well avoided looking at Ben; now I wanted to. I glanced surreptitiously at him. He was staring across the room, absently holding the steaming mug in one hand. I was hoping to see a man who wasn't lovable after all. Just an ordinary man you'd meet any day. He wasn't fond of me and had told me so. I was determined to see that I hadn't lost much. I looked at him hopefully.

Nothing had changed. Not a thing. He was as curiously attractive as ever, his thick hair untidy and overlong, his powerful plump body relaxed, his face a mixture of toughness and good nature. If anything, he had a certain added radiance because now he was unobtainable. It seemed extraordinary, when I looked at this cool cheerful man, to remember how passionately we'd kissed and how he'd closed his eyes, opening them again with such a conscious, tender glance. The difference between sex and no sex struck me then. How close you are. And then there's nothing. He caught my eyes and I blushed crimson.

Ignoring the blush he said:

'Your father will have to use his understudy to-morrow. *That* won't please him very much!'

'He's got a good one,' I muttered.

'What actor cares about that?' said Ben. 'He won't like it, and nor will the audience. There'll be a lot of groaning and asking for money back when they see that paper slip in the programme.'

We walked back down the passage into the hall, Sheba padding beside us.

When we were at the front door he turned.

'Off to bed with you! And stop looking so woe-begone. It's all okay now. Chris Laurie will be back to see your father in the morning, and all *you've* got to do is get some sleep and forget you had a scare. You've had a shock. You must look after yourself. Remember? I've told you that before.'

He spoke as if he were an elderly friend of my father's, an uncle perhaps. The tone was friendly and unselfconscious. I could not bear it. When he held out his hand I barely touched it.

He smiled.

'I'm glad your Dad didn't spring this a few days ago. On the night I saw *The Cherry Orchard*.'

'Oh. You saw it.'

'Your father was quite right,' he said, looking down at me without much expression. 'You are an artist.'

He left me.

# 9

Tam was furious when she heard about the night's drama; she had arrived back from a party only a few minutes after Ben had driven away.

Dr. Laurie called next morning before I was up, pronounced my father to be on the mend, and ruled that he was to stay in bed for two days.

Father, white in the face and handsome in a haggard way ('The Death of Chatterton,' he said, looking at himself in a hand mirror), rang the bell all day, made people scurry up and downstairs like palace courtiers, demanded strange food, and tormented Mrs. Brown by forcing her to type on a tray on her lap in his bedroom.

Tam came into my dressing-room that evening during the performance of *The Cherry Orchard*. For quite a long period I wasn't on stage, and Tam had timed her arrival correctly. It was her dressing-room as well as mine, we did not play in the same production, and we alternated in using the room. Our six costumes (four of mine for Russian Anya; two of hers for French

Midinette) hung on a long rail in the corner, alongside those belonging to Periandra, for it was her room too. This was Dad's idea: 'You'll learn from Peachey. Everybody does.'

'I want to know *exactly* how you felt when you opened the front door and saw Ben again,' Tam said sitting on the table, her back against my first-night greetings telegrams stuck in the edge of the mirror.

'I didn't feel a thing. I was too frightened. Just grateful Ben found the doctor. You can't imagine how ill Dad looked.'

'Dad ill!' mused Tam. She'd been chewing over the event all day. 'I can't imagine it. He's as strong as an ox.'

'Your father is no such thing,' said Periandra rustling into the dressing-room. She wore the satisfied air, a cheerful halo, of an actress whose exit has just been applauded. She was dressed in her Charlotta, Act II, costume: straw boater dead straight on top of straw-blonde wig, checked hunting suit with buttons on the sleeves, chalky face. Her eagle's nose poked out from beneath the hat brim as if she were going to eat one of us.

'*I* should know about Sir if anyone should,' she said, speaking to herself in the mirror. 'I have played with your father more than any other actress in London. He has a delicate constitution. He conceals it from you girls.

He doesn't want to alarm you. But he's as highly-strung as a violin — he vibrates. And that vibration can be unbearable. I am exactly the same,' she said, sitting down, her knees apart under the long skirt, and giving her head a good scratch.

'I meant he was physically strong, and so he is,' said Tam, never impressed by Periandra as I was. 'He can fence and wrestle and fight better than any member of the company. He's as strong as an ox. Of course he's got temperament. So he ought: he's an actor.'

'He's not *an* actor, he's *the* actor,' snapped Periandra. 'Off with you, Tamara. When you're not playing, you're like a mosquito about the place. Too much of your company and we will be covered in bites! You may not believe it, but your sister requires quiet during a performance. As I do.'

She waved the surprised Tam straight out of the dressing-room.

Periandra and I sat listening to the actors' voices over the intercom in a blessed silence. The play surrounded us. It was odd, but as I sat there with her, I knew she was absolutely right.

★ ★ ★

241

My father returned to health and his role of Gayev. He couldn't wait to stop the understudy earning another evening's extra pay, let alone that scatter of kindly applause given to understudies bravely filling gaps. Dad was as full of vitality as ever, but had no intention of letting us forget his indisposition. He prefaced his more monstrous demands with, 'What I need after that terrible Experience of My Illness . . .'

Life settled down, if you could call anything settled with my father around. My success levelled out too. Now and again journalists still asked for interviews, and these usually went to a pattern. A talk with me. A carefully-arranged photo call, with Dad and Tam included if this could be managed (Dad was often unobtainable, Tam never). Shots of us usually by the fireplace or reflected in a full-length mirror. Shots of me on a bicycle in the garden. Shots of us at the stage door of the Royalty. Shots of Tam and me with Sheba as a valuable, always obliging prop.

Dad was in the throes of planning sessions: plays had to be worked out months in advance and casting was full of frustrations. 'Actors, actors,' Dad sometimes groaned. It always meant the same thing: that he had just lost someone to movies or to rivals.

However busy he was, my father was restive

for enjoyment on Sundays when the weather was fine. He had two ways of enjoying himself. The first was hiring an electric punt at Wargrave and taking Tam and me miles down the river: we liked those days on the water; we explored backwaters thick with flowering weed, and chugged gently past houses sloping to the river's edge like Toad Hall; sometimes we picked water lilies. Then there was Dad's other way.

Mrs. Brown came into the garden one sunny Sunday morning when Tam and I were sitting in the shade of the crab-apple tree. Faces made brown or reddened by sunshine were despised by my father, who said that healthy-looking actresses should be condemned to play only Brechtian peasants.

'Sir Robert says will you get ready, please,' said Mrs. Brown, coming across the grass.

'And what exactly does that mean?' asked Tam.

'A picnic out of doors, I believe.'

'We didn't expect he'd take us to Simpson's, and give us hot roast beef,' said Tam rather rudely. 'But is it the river, Mrs. Brown? Or Dad in his role of Proust?'

'My father sometimes feels a remembrance of things past and takes us to look at his old school,' I translated.

'If it was only his old school!' said Tam.

'What about the Painted Hall at Greenwich where he learned 'officer-like qualities' in that old nineteen-forty war? Or Nelson's *Victory* where some idiot once let him sleep in a hammock, condemning us to everlasting pilgrimage . . . '

'And the flat at Worthing . . . '

'And the house in Brixton where his granny lived . . . '

'I should have thought,' said Mrs. Brown with growing disapproval, 'you would have been interested and proud to see where Sir Robert passed the time when he was young.'

'Take no notice of us, Mrs. Brown, and do try and find out whether it's the river or not,' I said. She gave us a cool look and went back to the house.

My father was already at the wheel of the car, happy and expectant, while Harriet stowed baskets of food in the boot.

'All set? Fine. In you get, girls. Now for a treat.'

We drove down to the country with the windows open, my father singing in a reedy voice strangely thin for an instrument able to vibrate drama round the world.

I was in front with Dad, Tam in the back of the car, leaning forward to join in the conversation. Dad didn't tell us where we were going until we were well past Windsor.

'Put us out of our misery. Is it your birthplace?' inquired Tam.

'Aha.'

'Dad, do tell,' I said as Tam groaned.

'I thought we'd go and take a peep at my village school,' Dad said. 'You'll like that. You've seen St. Edmund's where I went when I was twelve but I've never taken you to the little school where I started at only five years old. I was quite a star pupil, of course. I carved my name on the desk. Wouldn't it be fun if it was still there?'

'Hysterical,' said Tam.

'I'll tell you something else. I thought we'd go and see where my old dentist lived. Do you remember I told you about him? He had a wooden leg.'

'Have mercy, Dad!'

He went on singing.

We picnicked in a beech-wood, and after we'd had coffee and Tam had climbed a tree and my father had proved that he could stand on his head longer than I could and that it definitely cleared the brain, we set off to find the school, after parking the car on a small common.

Dad loped about, looking over hedges and gates and walking boldly into gardens which I prayed were deserted. He exclaimed at everything he saw, turning to us with the perfect confidence of a man who knew you must be as riveted with interest as he.

'There's the tree where I made a tree-house. On that thick branch over there. I was a touching child.'

Did we see that shed by the hedge? He'd fallen off it and hurt his back. And that whitewashed place which looked so camp with the purple door? It was a workman's cottage in his day, and the old gardener who lived there had taught him carpentry.

'Did I show you the cupboard I made?'

'Yes, Dad, I've still got it,' I said (and many times had to hide it from designers re-doing the house).

'Well, of course, it should be kept. My dovetailing was remarkable for a boy of my age.'

We found the school, a low pink brick building at the corner of the common. 'That's the place. Imagine, *I* learned to read in that very room over there.'

Tam and I exchanged glances as he went over and pressed his face against the window.

He turned to us with an amazed expression.

'They've changed it. It isn't a school at all. WHERE IS MY DESK?'

We joined him at the window and looked into a big whitewashed room, lined with

246

shelves of bright paperbacks. The room, empty of people, had black leather furniture, white fur rugs and Japanese posters.

'They've turned My school into that — that stage set,' he said. Astonished and indignant, he marched back to the car.

'Let's go and find the dentist,' I suggested comfortingly.

Dad cheered up when we located a small shop, with a flat above it, and a brass plate which read 'M. Shipman, L.D.S., R.C.S.'

'The very same man!' he cried.

'Dad! It can't be. He'd be nearly eighty,' I said.

My father hesitated, peered at the brass plate again.

'Well, it could be his son. But it's nice to know they're still at it. He crowned this molar, you know,' pointing at one of his splendid teeth. 'It was chipped at football.'

The continued existence of M. Shipman, L.D.S., R.C.S., restored my father's faith in humanity, and on the way home he recited for our entertainment long pieces of dialogue remembered from ancient Will Hay films.

★ ★ ★

During the following days Tam, who threw off sore throats in twenty-four hours and disappointments in a little more, was quite recovered from her glassy brightness over my good notices. She was busy rehearsing a television play, full of her own affairs and the success of Johnnie Buckingham's art show, which had been given some coverage in the newspapers, the Press being friendly to twenty-one-year-old painters. Quite a number of the pictures had been sold (at considerably lower prices than Tam had labelled them), and Johnnie had been offered five pounds for 'Hot Sun Strike Twelve.'

I was not looking forward to the film test that had been fixed for me. Periandra, who never made films (Tam said it was because the camera elongated her nose) had rather alarmed me with advice. My father, reading my thoughts during dinner one night, said: 'Tests are nothing. Any girl making a chocolate commercial does them. Bones. That's all that matters. Bones. And you have Mine,' he added with satisfaction.

I came home from shopping on the afternoon before the film test, and when I let myself into the house I could hear the usual sound, my father's voice sonorously dictating to Mrs. Brown. Ventura was squatting in the hall, oiling the leaves of a large green plant by the staircase. When she saw me, she said something strange. She said: 'Oh, thank God,' and closed her eyes.

Drama was our daily bread and I smiled, unconcerned.

'I've been waiting for you. A long time. I could not tell Sir Robert,' Ventura said, her Italian accent made more strong by emotion.

'What is it, Ventura?'

'Harriet has gone.'

'Where?'

'She took luggage. Left the house.'

'Oh, rubbish!' I said, laughing. Ventura got to her feet and tugged my arm, pulling me up the stairs. There was nothing to do but follow.

Harriet's room was at the end of the passage on the same floor as Tam's and mine. It was a room we rarely visited. Tam had once called it 'Harriet's shrine' — even as children we were not encouraged to go there. Now it seemed an impertinence to barge in without knocking.

Ventura threw open the door and cried 'Look!'

The room was bare. Hair-brushes, make-up, the silver ink-stand, the picture of a children's ballet group with herself as a seven-year-old crowned with rosebuds, the photographs of Dad with Tam and me, everything had vanished. On the mantelpiece there had always been a glass-fronted jeweller's box that my father had brought her back from New York; it had held a single pearl. That was gone too. The empty room was tidy, bare and cold.

I went to the dressing-table and opened the drawer. In it was nothing but a solitary hairpin, lying on the lining-paper, for which Harriet had used one of my father's old programmes. Drawing-pinned together, the scarlet pages repeated 'Robert Waring, Robert Waring,' over and over.

Ventura and I went round the room uselessly, as if expecting to find Harriet behind a chair. I looked at the bed. Its cover was smooth and on the pillow was an envelope, white on white.

'Sir Robert, Candida and Tamara Waring,' was written on it in Harriet's bold old-fashioned writing.

The letter began without preliminaries:

'Forgive me for doing this. I've thought a lot and it is the only possible thing. If I had told you, you would all have tried to dissuade me. And if I tell you where I'm going now you'll come to find me. I don't want that. Please understand. Please do.

'I have decided on this move and I mean it. I must work things out for myself from now on.

'This letter is collective because it's all

three of you, the family, that I'm losing and I can't separate you when I say good-bye. I suppose I can't say good-bye either because you all live in me and so I can't lose you. I love you dearly. Please forgive me.

'Harriet.'

In the study, my father was sitting with Hal Adams, one of his associate directors, deep in work. Schedules, manuscripts, designs, papers, lay everywhere. Books were piled in heaps on the floor. Mrs. Brown was doing what she called a 'flow chart' of repertory performances, pinned on a large drawing-board. As I came into the room all three of them turned, three pairs of eyes wore the look that said 'What the hell does she want?' But my father, after one quick glance, said: 'Wait in the drawing-room. I'm coming.'

I went into the drawing-room and a moment later he came quickly in, closing the door.

'What's happened, Puss?'

I gave him the letter. As he came towards me his expression was lustrous, absent, as it often was when he was deeply absorbed in work, it had a sort of far-off shine. As he read the letter, the brightness went. He put his arm round my shoulders and we went over to the settee and sat down together.

'What do you know about this, Candida?'

'Nothing. Nothing.'

'Are you quite sure?'

'Of course! Of course I am. It's mad. Crazy. People like Harriet, I mean a whole great lump of one's life, don't just disappear. They can't.'

'It seems that they do.'

He appeared to be expecting something from me.

'Dad,' I said solemnly, 'I've been thinking. It was because we swallowed her, wasn't it? We all did. We took everything. She's not young and she's given us all her life and I suppose she wanted to be free. It was brave to go.'

My father listened to this with a sardonic face. He dropped his eyelids.

'Candida, Candida,' he said, shaking his head and sighing. 'What it is to be twenty. Can you really sit there and tell me that Harry went because we used up her time, that *I* used up her time! Do you suppose Harry would think anything so mawkish? What better way could she spend her time, pray? She's in trouble, that's what this is about. Real trouble. And she's hiding it, from Me.'

He looked down at the letter and read it again. Now and again he read a phrase aloud, his head on one side, like a man tuning a piano. 'It's the only possible thing. Could she mean . . . ' he murmured.

After a while he folded the letter and put it in his wallet. He turned to me kindly.

'You're not to fret, Puss. It's nothing to do with you. I've been too busy, too wrapped up in the company. The Ghilain; *The Orchard*; Gayev; launching you. I blame myself. I should have seen how it was with Harry. Good God, it must have been sticking out a mile. Are you sure you don't know anything? You're quite a perceptive creature. Come along, now, *think*.'

Then I remembered Jack Swift.

My father asked a lot of questions, looked pleased, kissed me and told me to go. Wasn't I due at the film test? He'd see me there. I was to do nothing about Harriet except tell Tamara.

'Tell her from me to spare us the big scene,' he said, turning at the door to wink, with quite his customary panache.

Mrs. Brown drove with me to the film studio. She was pretty quiet during the drive. I didn't know if Dad had told her anything, he probably hadn't for he was bossy and never intimate in his dealings with her. But she looked subdued and I was selfishly glad not to have to talk to her. Mrs. Brown's conversation was always the same: a rehash of Dad's current opinions without the pepper.

My father joined us as the film test was being shot. I was nervous and glad to see him. While a make-up girl was retouching my face before they started shooting again, I looked over at him talking to a young film director and making him laugh. He looked so relaxed and important that I thought: 'I won't worry about Harriet. I won't worry about anything. There's nothing Dad can't do.' I believed his legend too.

When the test was over we were given tea, and shown to the car as if we were visiting royalty. Dad hummed a tune while we were driving back.

'Shall I go into the theatre and tell Tam the news before she comes home?' I said, after a pause in which Dad continued to hum heartlessly. I did not know why he was cheerful; my adoring admiration disappeared.

'Yes, it's less depressing than the child arriving to find Harriet missing,' said Dad. 'Good idea. Mind you wait till the end of the performance before telling her or you'll throw her.'

'I wouldn't *dream* . . . ' I began huffily.

'Why not?' demanded my father. 'I knew a leading actress who broke off an affair between the acts of a Coward revival. And

254

very *unfunny* she was in the second half. Ruined my best bits. Don't be holy, Puss. Things sometimes do happen during the performance. I am merely suggesting you don't make them.'

It was ten minutes before the end of the play when I arrived at the Royalty that night. The foyer had the empty yet peopled look of a theatre crammed to the roof inside; a foyer with no single person in view but a tired commissionaire still has an unmistakable aura when there's a packed house.

I went round to the stage door. Sid, who had taken a fancy to me since he'd won on a horse called Candy Bar, shouted Hallo how was I and very good luck to me, rather as if I were galloping past the post myself.

I went up to our dressing-room. There was no sign of my sister, but Periandra was there, flirting. To-night, exquisite in the costume as a French marquise, she was in blue, silver and diamonds. To-night's man was Mike, a tough young actor who played murderers, boxers and roughnecks on stage and a dove off-stage if Periandra was about.

'I've told the director again and again . . . ' Periandra was saying. She stopped as I came in.

'Candida. You never call on a Ghilain night. How nice. Mike, leave us!'

He shrugged and lounged out.

Periandra tightened an enormous diamond earring more firmly and glanced at me. She had Jewish blood, and this intensified her large swimming eyes.

'Why have you come round?' she asked at once.

'Something's happened I have to tell Tam.'

'Indeed?'

Who could refuse news to Periandra? She always got it anyway. Like the eagle, she was never hungry if she could help it.

'Harriet's gone. Disappeared.'

'Gentle heaven!' exclaimed Periandra, with her involuntary mimicry of my father's voice.

She listened to my story, now and again interrupting warmly. It was terrible, she said, terrible. And yet . . . I had an odd feeling. I was sure Periandra already knew what had happened. Was it because I was an actress myself that I felt the nuance of a performance in her? Something slightly overdone, just too right . . .

'Tam's due in a moment,' she said. We heard the voices and a wave of laughter. 'That's her exit line. She's off now.'

Tam came quickly into the room and I had that split second that every bearer of bad news knows, thinking 'Now she's still happy.'

When I told her what had happened she

began to cry. I went over and put my arms round her; that made her sob louder.

Periandra said impatiently, 'Leave her alone. Leave her to me. Stop it, Tamara. Stop that bawling and listen.'

Tam looked up, her face streaked and sad, as Periandra pointed to the intercom. We heard words coming up to the end of the play.

'You have exactly one minute to do your face before the curtain!' Periandra said.

Tam ran to the looking-glass and fiercely mopped her face, patting powder under the eyes. Looking at me in the glass she said:

'Johnnie's out front and he's coming for me. Don't wait. I'd rather go with him. Please.'

Periandra stood up as we heard the first breaking wave of applause.

'Tamara. Come,' she said, striding out like a swimmer going towards the sea.

★　★　★

While the sound of clapping still rose and fell I went out of the theatre to where the car was waiting. Harris, my father's chauffeur, opened the door for me. I thanked him, hoping as with Mrs. Brown, that I wasn't going to be talked to.

'Traffic's very bad,' he said as we began the drive towards home. 'Impossible to park. Had to cruise round all the time so as not to miss you. Shocking.'

It never worked with Dad, but perhaps he thought it was worth trying with me.

'You have a nerve-racking job,' I said dutifully. 'It gets worse all the time.' If the words had been spoken by Dad they would have pleased Harris very much. He'd always been a fan. It was a shame that they only came from me, and even as I said them I knew they didn't really count. He drove in silence after that and I stared out of the window and thought about Periandra.

I was more and more convinced that she'd known about Harriet before I told her. It wasn't in her face, usually inscrutable because the feelings shown were those she put there. But in her manner there had been the merest hint of completeness, rather as if she'd eaten and you had not.

Harriet and Periandra had been grudging friends for years. Harriet was rude about her, scornfully dismissing her claim to have been a ballet dancer, jeering at her flirtations with boys of nineteen. It made Harriet laugh to watch Periandra, when she was at her most girlish, suddenly turn into the queen regent. Harriet respected her talent and liked

Periandra's friendliness and curiosity. Periandra was just the person to confide in. Like many gossipy people, she could be completely secret when she chose.

The windows at home were shining in the dusk and when I went indoors there were voices in the drawing-room. I pushed open the double doors. Dad was sitting in a high-backed chair, smoking a cheroot. Facing him was Jack Swift.

'You know Mr. Swift, I believe,' said Dad, with a wave of his hand. 'Sit down, Candida. You have come at the right time.'

'Surprised to see me?' asked Jack Swift, very much at home. 'Sir Robert telephoned. Asked me to pop round. Yours to command, I said.' Then, to me, 'How's instant stardom? I saw you on the box the other night.'

'Mr. Swift isn't exactly here to pay us a social call,' drawled my father. 'He tells me that he can help us with our inquiries.'

'Quite right. Quite correct. I said a little more than that, though. I said I could help at a price,' said Swift, laughing.

'So you did,' said my father.

Swift stared back boldly. His shrewd shifty face was alert; he had dark eyes. He was respectably dressed in a rather old-fashioned blue suit, a woven tie and dirty shoes. He reminded me of a retired boxer who'd fallen on hard times, but whose brains had remained intact.

My father looked Swift up and down again, his manner deliberately insulting, his eyes narrowed. The other man, practised too, continued to sip his drink in comfort.

He pointed to me. 'Better if she isn't here, you know.'

'My daughter and I have no secrets.'

'Oh yes you have.'

'What does that mean?'

'You'd be surprised what secrets you've got. Nice expensive ones as far as I'm concerned. Are you sure you want her here?'

My father suddenly looked as if he wanted to hit him.

'Out with it,' he said, biting off the words.

'Okay, okay, your funeral. You want me to spill the beans, I'll spill them. Don't say I didn't warn you. I have documents in my possession. Letters. All photos, of course. To prove that your cook-housekeeper is your sister.'

The moment after Jack Swift said that extraordinary thing there was complete silence. My father froze.

'Surprise, surprise,' said Swift, breaking into the hush. 'Your sister. How about that! Half-sister, to be exact. Your dad's illegit. Little bastard he had by a ballet dancer in the nineteen-twenties. Remember you met her with your father while you were still at drama school? Oh yes, I know all about it. Quite good at digging up the facts when I'm interested. The first time you met her, you were being introduced to your kid sister! And after you married, wasn't it your father who suggested you give Harriet a job? She was in the ballet but not doing too well. Fell for the leading male dancer, who didn't want to know, and your dad suggested you could help her out, give her a job for a bit . . . '

'How long has Harriet known?' my father asked with a slight shudder.

'Matter of weeks. Quite a shock for her really. She wouldn't believe it at first, but then I came up with the evidence. Incontrovertible. There it was in black and white.' Swift's manner, with an affectation of ease until now, was changing. My father walked over to the window and turned his back. Swift looked at that back, then spoke to me.

'Good story, wouldn't you think?' he said, grinning without showing his teeth. 'I dare say you've read some of those Sunday stories in the more *popular* papers — love stories with a difference. Sail pretty near to the wind. Libel, you'd say; not a bit of it. Papers have their tame lawyers. Everything's vetted and above-board. Of course it has to be professionally written, and be sympathetic, you know what I mean? A tender secret in the life of the great actor . . . that kind of thing. Touch the beating heart of the public. Nothing dirty. A juicy sentimental steak for Sunday dinner with the veg and chips. Might get a packet for it if I turned it into a series. Friend of mine ghosted one called 'I was a Nun at Sixteen.' Got fourteen thousand quid. Of course your father could buy it instead. Nothing easier.'

I didn't say a thing, but just looked at the white face with its spiteful confidence, and the dark eyes cosily looking into mine. My father's back was still turned to us, his hands clasped behind him.

At last he turned round and began to move towards us, walking slowly.

He spoke in a soft, purring voice.

'You sell that story to a newspaper. You just do that. And I'll make a public statement about your blackmail that will put you in prison for fifteen years. I'll make you sorry you've been born. Do you think you can threaten Me? You'll be old when you get out of gaol. Do you know that? You'll be old. Go on now. Off with you. Go and sell Harriet's story and don't say,' his voice was rising in power, '*you haven't been warned.*'

He looked like a stalking animal and as he

came up to Swift, I really thought he'd pounce. I literally thought Dad might kill him.

Swift was as frightened as I. He jumped to his feet, gabbling something I couldn't hear, and ran out of the room. The front door slammed.

There was a long pause. Dad turned round to me and suddenly laughed.

'Not bad, eh? My Iago bit.'

He sat down next to me and I gripped his arm.

'That's taken care of him very nicely. Very nicely,' he said.

He was silent for a while and then spoke in quite a different voice. 'So Harry's my sister. Well, well. And that's why she's run away. Silly old girl. Silly woman. Where are we going to find her, mm?'

'I think Periandra knows . . . ' I whispered.

# 10

I'd had enough. I'd had quite enough. A few days ago I had thought my father was going to die; Ben had turned up with the doctor in the middle of the night. Then we'd lost Harriet. Now this. Melodrama was too much for me and the only way of escape was to go to bed.

Tam came into my room very late. My light was still on and I was trying to read. She sat on the bed and I told her the news briefly, while she stared, her mouth open with amazement.

'So Dad's gone off to bully Periandra now,' I finished. 'I hope to God I'm right and she does know something. Otherwise where will he look for Harriet? Where do you find people in this huge great town?'

All Tam managed was 'Crumbs.'

She hadn't washed her face properly after the performance, there were crimson dots at the corners of her eyes and broad black marks above and below the lids. She had a faint look of Midinette, as if something of the farce were hanging round: leftover laughs gone cold.

'Don't worry,' I said, looking at the frivolous face in profile. 'You're always telling me Dad can't help winning.'

'I couldn't bear it if he didn't win this time,' she said, with a sobbing sigh.

She began to talk about Harriet, a thing she never did any more than she talked about sleeping or eating. Now and again as she danced through the days she would comment that Harriet was 'mean,' Tam's word for someone not giving her her own way. But to-night with Harriet lost, the taking-for-granted was gone too and she spoke of Harriet as if of a mother.

'It was different for you,' Tam said to me. It was true. I'd known my own mother a little, but Tam couldn't remember anyone but Harriet. Harriet was the one she could talk to when everything was a mess. She didn't hurt me by this. It had always been true. As she talked, my sister never actually mentioned that Harriet herself might be unhappy.

'Dad will find her, won't he?' she repeated hungrily, waiting for good news.

But to-night I couldn't give it to her. I didn't want to. I'd always been good at handing out a meaningless optimism to my sister. When she was a child it had been a pleasure to do so. I had loved to see her beaming face. And when she grew up I was stuck with giving Tam a sugary 'happy end' to our conversations.

Now, when Tam waited for her helping of sugar I was worrying, instead, about the possibility of my father having to look for Harriet in the miles and miles of streets outside in the dark. For suppose my idea failed and Periandra couldn't help? What else could he do? I was sure he wouldn't go to the police. That was the disadvantage of having a face as familiar as Nelson's.

After a while Tam went and fetched some hot milk. We sat cradling the mugs in our hands. It was long after midnight.

'I'm a selfish bitch,' Tam said suddenly.

I'd been thinking just that, so of course I said she wasn't.

'I haven't asked you anything about yourself. How is it? With Ben, I mean.'

'I'm getting over it. It was never a great love, you know.'

We waited for the telephone and it didn't ring. We listened for voices and they didn't echo up the stairs. We opened the door so as not to miss a sound and what seeped in was silence. The night dragged on. We were quiet and tingling with nerves when there was the noise of a slamming car door. We rushed to the window.

'It's them — there's Dad!' cried Tam. 'He's

got a suitcase. Oh! oh! there she is!'

They were in the hall as Tam and I came hammering down the stairs, jumping the last few steps. No one said a thing.

★ ★ ★

'Sir said I must wake you or you'll sleep away your brains,' said a voice.

Curtains were pulled and the light came in rather suddenly.

I sat up yawning. Harriet was standing at the end of my bed, dressed in her white overall, sleeves rolled up, face calm.

'Ow. Harriet! Does your head ache as badly as mine?'

'It aches a little.'

'How much champagne did we drink, do you suppose?' I groaned. 'When I think how Dad usually hides the drink from us . . . I don't remember much, do you?'

'The jokes.'

I struggled up against the pillows while Harriet put the tray on my lap. Through hangover and tiredness, I too remembered Dad's jokes. He had been at his impossible-to-resist, and the four of us had laughed so much that Tam, doubled up, at one time had to stagger into the next room to recover.

'You're my *aunt*,' I said at last, looking up.

'*What* about that!' she said, laughing.

She looked quite approachable this morning, and while I drank coffee but refused anything to eat I felt I could ask a little about Jack Swift.

'Was it awful while it was all happening?'

'It was, rather. I was a fool to believe he'd do what he said. I suppose that's how blackmailers work. Sir says Swift would never have got away with it. But all the time I was sure he would. Peachey Pratt was a help. A real mate.'

'A real nosy-parker.'

'No, no, Candida,' Harriet said. 'She loves a bit of excitement but she's loyal. It's what's attractive about her. And it thrilled her to do something for Sir.'

'You will *have* to stop calling him that.'

Harriet raised her eyebrows. Her face was still the tragic muse's outside the Royalty theatre. Its lines, like those of the Italian actor Vagnoli, were made by the bones beneath the yellowish skin, and by the way her cheeks creased when she smiled or frowned. It was a sad face by accident, really.

'I told your father when he came to Peachey's last night that I'd only come back on my own terms. He was so quixotic, Candy! He was for making a press announcement. The newly-discovered sister.

Imagine how the pro's would laugh at *that*. He got quite swept away and wanted to spend ridiculous sums of money on me — clothes and mink and a lot of old stuff like that.'

'He didn't offer you cash!'

'Of course he didn't. He said I could put it on his account.'

'But how lovely — we can — '

'No, we can't. I'd feel stupid dressed up as Sir's rich sister. I have far more power in my overall, my girl, than I'd have disguised in dowager's mink.'

She walked over to rearrange the curtain folds so that they were symmetrical, and then leaned out of the window and said, had I noticed the flowering currant?

Speaking to her back, which reminded me of Dad's, I said:

'Harriet.'

'What is it?'

'One more thing.'

She came back and sat down on the bed, looking at me with a benevolent expression that usually preceded her announcing that she'd got work to do.

'There's something I don't understand. I remember thinking it last night now and then when Dad wasn't making us laugh, and again just now. You'd say you had a strong will, wouldn't you? Tam and I always say you have.'

'Stubborn as a mule.'

'I agree! So how did Dad get you to change your mind? I can't think he just said he'd told Swift to get out and you might as well pack your suitcase and come back. It's too simple. After making such a big decision . . . '

She said musingly, 'It's odd you should ask. I thought of it myself when I woke this morning. I opened my eyes and saw I was here and not at Peachey's and lay thinking about Sir arriving last night and all we'd said.'

'Was he very persuasive?'

She looked at me vaguely. 'Not a bit. He just talked, rather quietly. Do you know, Candy, he seemed so tired. It sounds silly. But he looked as if he'd shrunk.'

★   ★   ★

All during a day flat with anticlimax but comfortable as old clothes, I thought about what Harriet had said. Her words were bits of jigsaw and I put them next to pieces of my own. What word had she used? When she talked with Dad last night he seemed 'as if he'd shrunk.' It was the exact thing I'd noticed about him, another night, when he had asked me to act again. It had hurt me to see that he wasn't young and strong any more. He'd looked diminished.

Dad had once told me that no actor could be great unless in his performance he had a matching capacity to be hurt. He must be able to be wounded, seem vulnerable; the audience would sense this and love him because of it. My father was a great actor, how often did he use that power? And use it on me?

That evening I went into his study before dinner to put back some books and found him alone. He was seated by the window on the green taffeta settee, books piled round him, Sheba lying at his feet like a dog in some Victorian painting: 'The Joys of Home.'

'Hallo, Puss,' my father said. 'Life is settled down again, you see. High time. I have to start on the Greek film and the next few weeks are going to be tough. How is it with you?'

'How is it with *you*, Dad?'

'If you are inquiring about my health, it is excellent,' he replied, his voice changing to match mine, which had not been particularly friendly. 'Laurie came in this morning to give me a check-up. I gather that admirer of yours is still sponging on him.'

'You'll be relieved to hear, since you dislike journalists, that he isn't an admirer

271

any more,' I replied tartly.

My father assumed the astounded expression he wore if anyone answered him sharply. His jaw dropped and he purposely exaggerated the face he was making. But I refused to laugh. The reference to Ben had annoyed me.

'My ankle is giving me trouble,' he said, giving up the grimace when the audience didn't react. 'I have to jump thirty feet in the new movie. Don't want any of the old bother with it.'

Here was a subject of real interest to him, unlike the reference to some man he had half forgotten. He stuck his foot out in front of him, using Sheba as a footstool, and waggled it, looking solemnly at his ankle.

I went over and knelt at his feet as I had done many times as a child. It had been a joke between us. My father would always say, 'That is right, that is where you belong.' I took the foot in both hands, supported it and began to massage. My father enjoyed this and stayed still while I kneaded and rubbed.

'Dad. Will you tell me something?'

'Don't rub too hard. To the left, to the left.'

'There's something I want to ask you.'

'Yes, that's just the spot. Easy now. Ah, that's wonderful,' he said, closing his eyes blissfully.

'It's about Harriet.'

'You're rather good at massage, Candida. I'd forgotten what strong fingers you have.' I pinched him slightly. He opened his eyes. 'What about Harry?' he asked, looking down at my kneeling figure.

'I thought it was brilliant, the way you got her back.'

He looked pleased and melted into a smile.

'How did you do it, Dad?'

'Ah, we don't reveal our secrets; we keep our mystery,' he said. 'But I'll admit it was quite a little performance. But I longed to have dear old Harry back. I was determined to get her, too. So I projected a bit. Just a bit.'

I went on massaging.

'Yes, it was good,' said Dad, as if he were in an art gallery standing away from a masterpiece to get it in the right light. He actually put his head on one side, murmuring, 'A bit of art.'

I dropped his foot with a thump.

'You *are* a *monster*!' I shouted.

'Of course. And a genius too,' agreed my father. I went out of the room thoughtfully, walked down the corridor deep in thought, and came face to face with Ben Nash.

It was a shock. My hands went cold.

'Hallo,' he said easily. 'I'm here to see your father. The mag's doing international theatre and I want to talk to him about that Italian company — isn't it the della Robbia? — who are coming over to the Royalty. Mrs. Brown fixed for me to have a word. Is he okay? Chris Laurie said he was visiting here to-day.'

'Only his ankle,' I answered briefly.

'Sprained?'

'Four years ago.'

It was an effort, but I managed to smile, and Ben laughed.

'Come into the drawing-room and I'll see if he can see you now,' I said.

The french windows were open on to the garden, and Sheba lolloped in, saw Ben and thumped her tail. This sign of recognition, making Ben the old friend he was not, seemed more painful than anything else. I was in a bad way, and I hurried out of the room, annoyed with myself.

My father wasn't in the study, and when I found Harriet in the kitchen she informed me that he was having a bath.

'He'll be hours. He wants to relax and he says the hot water's good for his ankle. Is it Ben Nash, by the way?' she said, looking at me quickly. 'Would you rather I saw him for you?'

'Of course not.'

Ben was gazing at the garden when I came back into the drawing-room. He was standing just as my father had done last night. I

274

wondered why people's backs were touching.

'He's decided to have a bath. I really am sorry, but I think he imagined you were coming later,' I lied. 'Can you fix another time with Mrs. Brown?'

'Of course not.'

He moved over to say good-bye, actually stretching out his hand. It took a lot to speak to that face which hadn't a sign of meaning in it.

'I want to talk to you,' I said.

He looked at me, rather surprised, and I remember thinking again that his eyes were very blue; one of them had a flaw, like the flaws you see in china. I disliked him for looking cheerful.

'Wouldn't it be better if you didn't?' he said.

I blushed angrily. 'No, it wouldn't! It's a farce that we've never said a word about that meaningless letter of yours. You never told me what it was all about and I want to know. Now. I want you to tell me to my face why you threw me over.'

I was beginning to tremble.

'My dear girl, I didn't throw you over, as you call it.'

'Of course you did. That's exactly what you did. Why?'

I took a step towards him and suddenly I

knew that he couldn't stop coming near to me as well.

'Don't ask me, please,' he said.

Silence. In it flashed for me a sudden understanding.

'I don't have to ask you. I know! It was Dad.' I began to cry stormily, remembering my father's face and the voice saying 'I can do Everything.'

'It was Dad,' I sobbed. 'He asked you to leave me because it would damage my career!'

'So he's told you.'

'Of course he hasn't! He wants to keep you away for good. It's horrible of him. Horrible. I'll never forgive him. Why can't he leave me alone — I can't bear it . . .'

I was angry and upset and scarcely knew what I said. I found myself pressed in Ben's arms.

'How did he do it? What did he say to you? I must know, you owe it to me!' I added, crying harder.

He put his arms closer round me as if my sobs hurt him, and said that I'd guessed so much I might as well know the rest. My father had telephoned him before the first night and they'd had a long talk. Dad had said he was worried about me. He had asked Ben to come to the house.

'Where was I when you came?'

'I think you were asleep,' he said. 'It was just before the opening night. He impressed me, Candida. He was so fair. Kind. Rather touching, as a matter of fact.'

'Oh, I'm sure!'

'No, no, you must believe me. I'm used to dealing with people, and he impressed me. He told me something he'd never spoken about to you. That he believed one day you would — you will — be a fine actress, even a remarkable one. He believed you were going to succeed in *The Cherry Orchard*. And he said that in his own career he'd found good acting needed a cleared mind in which thoughts and feelings could find room and grow. He said you were new to it and needed that very badly. Stirring up real-life emotions could make the creative power dry up. He knew you.'

'What did that mean?'

'That actresses are emotional creatures and inclined to fall in love easily, sometimes even at a crucial point in their careers. He'd seen it before. You yourself had had crushes and now had a bit of one on me. If I was fond of you — and cared about your future — I'd keep away.'

We weren't pressed against each other any more, and when he spoke it was in the reasonable relaxed voice he'd used earlier. He sounded a good journalist and a kind man and that was all.

'Your father was right. You proved it. I'm glad for you.'

'Oh thanks.'

'Candida! Don't sound like that. I can't have you bitter about your father when he's done so much for you. When you mean so much to him.'

'And nothing to you.'

'Let's leave that bit.' He spoke as if he and I were standing by some crumbling wall where, years before, we'd hidden a towen, once touchingly full of meaning. 'We must leave that bit.'

He put his hand out in a kindly good-bye. I ignored it.

'Ben! Answer me something. Don't look martyred, I *will* open the subject again if I want to. Don't you like me at all? Don't you know how much I long to be with you . . . how much I miss you? How dare my father tell you I'm always falling for people. It's a lie and said to put you off, and very successful it proved. Don't I mean anything?'

And because I knew that by going close I could still have an effect, I moved very close although I did not touch him.

He didn't say a thing. His face changed

and I saw the look I thought I was never to see again. He put his arms round me and we began to kiss.

★ ★ ★

Harriet was making pastry in the absent manner of the professional, rolling and patting the dough. Tam was seated on a stool, legs at the right angle, pink trousers of the right cut. Both turned as I came into the kitchen, and looked at me.

'Don't tell us. Let us guess,' said Tam. 'Love is on again. See the lunch-time edition! 'Theatre Star's Daughter Surprise'.'

'Is it on again?' Harriet's voice was softer than usual and softer than Tam's.

'I suppose it is. And it isn't love. Maybe it won't be.'

Tam laughed. 'Be still, Thudding Heart! Of course it's love. I insist on it.'

I muttered that I just wanted to be around with Ben and that was what I was going to do from now on.

'Who's stopping you?' asked Tam airily. 'Where was I? Ah yes. Harriet, the *As You* casting isn't complete but they *can't* expect me to do Audrey if they give me Charles Keats as Touchstone. How could that sexy Audrey burst out of her dress over Charles

Keats? And talking of bursting out, don't I have to get a special bra to push my bosoms together?'

Tam and I went upstairs to change for luncheon. There was a small group of American actors and directors in London who had come over to study London's subsidised theatre. My father was entertaining them to-day.

'I plan to look my loveliest!' said Tam. 'I shall knock them cold in white. Why don't you do the same?'

I went into my room and opened the wardrobe and stood there but forgot that I was supposed to be changing my clothes. I thought of kissing Ben; and then I thought of love itself. And then I thought of acting. I wondered if my father was right and to play well I needed to be empty of strong feelings that were real. Was he saying that because we were actors, we were vessels waiting to be filled by false feelings, and our own made the liquid clouded or sour? It was a paradox that the opposite often happened — not that sex spoiled a performance, but that because of a particular play a pair of actors fell in love. I'd seen Rosalind and Orlando have a violent affair. I'd seen Cleopatra in the grip of powerfully real sex, and Kate helpless over Petruchio. It was something my father watched with knowledgeable amusement.

Tam soon came hammering at my door, dressed in a white shift, her hair glittering with lacquer. As she had suggested, we both wore white, and came down the stairs towards the familiar buzz of players all talking at once.

I rather liked our American visitors. They were a bit solemn, a bit holy, as my father would put it, and they used phrases like 'the continuing creativity of the arts' but they were eager and thoughtful and one or two of them looked like beautiful Red Indians. Hours went by. By the time lunch was over, and coffee was over, and after-coffee talk had spread out, it seemed as if the afternoon had gone on for ever. The yellow roses in the drawing-room, in bud when Ben had kissed me, were wide open in the heat and the smoke.

Our guests were scarcely able to tear themselves away from Dad, who'd decided to be his most fascinating. When they finally left it was after four in the afternoon. Dad closed the front door at last and gave a yawn like the yowl of a cat.

'No one should come to luncheon and stay for tea,' he said. 'Remember, girls. Always leave while your host is still pressing for you to stay.'

'And not shovelling you into your car,' said Tam.

'Too sharp, much too sharp,' said Dad, pinching her cheek. 'And fat. You need a workout, my girl. A track suit and a workout. I'll join you.'

Tam's face was an 'O' of horror. My father's workouts lasted three hours and reduced players to jelly. Theatre lore said actors broke legs, dislocated shoulders and slipped discs when invited to join my father's antics in the gym. Tam ran upstairs before he could say another word.

'That'll teach her to cheek me, eh, Puss?' said Dad, laughing at the retreating figure, and settling down for a chat.

'Sir Robert!' exclaimed Mrs. Brown, materialising from her office, 'I have a dozen messages.'

'All of which shall be dealt with immediately, Mrs. Brown! But you cannot keep me from My Child!' We strolled into the drawing-room.

The drawing-room was untidy, littered with traces of the thirty people who'd spent all afternoon here, from American cigarette packets to Pan Am. matches. The place smelled of yellow roses and smoke.

Dad threw himself on to the settee, lying among the cushions, both arms wide. He was very high-spirited.

'Come and sit by me, Puss. You look rather pretty. What's that word the critics used about you? Radiant. Why does my puss look radiant to-day?'

I sat down near him, but well out of arm's reach. I didn't intend to be folded in a fatherly embrace. Dad enjoyed kissing people, as most actors do. 'Some of us are born kissers,' he'd say with satisfaction, '*I* am the greatest of them all.' For this reason he would have no garlic used in the kitchen, and when anyone offered him food with onions in it he literally shuddered.

I looked over at him.

He returned the look with a sparkling face. Oh, that face. The long eyes were almond-shaped, and they made his face that of a hero: a Slav hero. There was a devilish look in it, you were never sure if it was going to melt or burn. His cheek-bones were high, the cheeks hollowed, and his beautiful mouth was so much larger than other people's. He grinned.

'I want to ask you a little question,' I said, light as a meringue.

'Ask away, Puss. Ask away.'

'You said it took a bit of art to get Harriet to come back.'

He chuckled reminiscently.

'That impressed you, didn't it? Yes. I moved

her. By God, I moved her. I moved myself too.'

'I bet you both cried.'

My father looked at me with surprise.

'I believe we did. Why not?'

'Nothing. I'm happy she's back and I'm glad you used your art,' I said. 'Dad. You remember when you persuaded me to come back to acting that night?'

Dad laughed outright. It was a real belly-laugh. 'Candy, Candy. You think I've been putting the 'fluence on you. Well, yes, I did. I wanted you in the company. I needed you. And *you* needed to do it . . . look how right I was. Am. So I gave you a little performance.'

I traced the pattern of the settee-cover with my finger and said casually:

'And you gave another to get rid of Ben Nash.'

I had to hand it to Dad. He didn't even blink. Actors have an iron control. When they dry, or when someone in the audience or the sky drops a tray or a thunderbolt, they don't move a muscle.

'Nash? Laurie's pal? The feller who wants to write about me?'

'Dad, *I know.*'

Pause.

'Oh. You do, eh? Who told you?'

I burst out, red from indigation: 'You're a monster. A monster. I like Ben. I think I even rather love him and what's more I'm going to see him all the time from now on and you're not going to stop me. *He* would never have told me what happened, but I guessed. I just knew — I know you, Dad! I know you too well. So don't you use that damned art of yours on me!'

'Bravo!' he cried, applauding. 'You did that very nicely. Your voice isn't quite low enough, we'll have to do something about its pitch.'

'Dad!'

'Daughter!'

He bridged the space between us then, put his arms round me and gave me such a smacking kiss that it echoed round the room.

'All right, all right, have your admirer if you must. But does he understand that he's dealing with a Waring? Does he know what he's up against?'

'He *loves* me being an actress.'

'Perhaps he does,' murmured my father, looking at me pensively. 'Perhaps he may be able to see that quality . . . All right, you have My permission to go around with him. But I don't promise not to knock his head off if he writes me an unintelligent notice.'

It was a waste of time telling Dad that Ben was not a critic.

My father stood up and stretched, looking nine feet tall. He bent down and pulled me to my feet.

'It's nice to see you happy, Puss.'

Just for a second, as the beautiful face looked down at me, emotion trembled across it like a breeze across water. Then he burst out laughing and I hit his shoulder with a clenched fist.

## THE END

## Other titles in the
## Ulverscroft Large Print Series:

## THE GREENWAY
## Jane Adams

When Cassie and her twelve-year-old cousin Suzie had taken a short cut through an ancient Norfolk pathway, Suzie had simply vanished . . . Twenty years on, Cassie is still tormented by nightmares. She returns to Norfolk, determined to solve the mystery.

## FORTY YEARS
## ON THE WILD FRONTIER
## Carl Breihan & W. Montgomery

Noted Western historian Carl Breihan has culled from the handwritten diaries of John Montgomery, grandfather of co-author Wayne Montgomery, new facts about Wyatt Earp, Doc Holliday, Bat Masterson and other famous and infamous men and women who gained notoriety when the Western Frontier was opened up.

## TAKE NOW, PAY LATER
## Joanna Dessau

This fiction based on fact is the love-turning-to-hate story of Robert Carr, Earl of Somerset, and his wife, Frances.

## McLEAN AT THE GOLDEN OWL
### George Goodchild

Inspector McLean has resigned from Scotland Yard's CID and has opened an office in Wimpole Street. With the help of his able assistant, Tiny, he solves many crimes, including those of kidnapping, murder and poisoning.

## KATE WEATHERBY
### Anne Goring

Derbyshire, 1849: The Hunter family are the arrogant, powerful masters of Clough Grange. Their feuds are sparked by a generation of guilt, despair and illfortune. But their passions are awakened by the arrival of nineteen-year-old Kate Weatherby.

## A VENETIAN RECKONING
### Donna Leon

When the body of a prominent international lawyer is found in the carriage of an intercity train, Commissario Guido Brunetti begins to dig deeper into the secret lives of the once great and good.

## A TASTE FOR DEATH
### Peter O'Donnell

Modesty Blaise and Willie Garvin take on impossible odds in the shape of Simon Delicata, the man with a taste for death, and Swordmaster, Wenczel, in a terrifying duel. Finally, in the Sahara desert, the intrepid pair must summon every killing skill to survive.

## SEVEN DAYS FROM MIDNIGHT
### Rona Randall

In the Comet Theatre, London, seven people have good reason for wanting beautiful Maxine Culver out of the way. Each one has reason to fear her blackmail. But whose shadow is it that lurks in the wings, waiting to silence her once and for all?

## QUEEN OF THE ELEPHANTS
### Mark Shand

Mark Shand knows about the ways of elephants, but he is no match for the tiny Parbati Barua, the daughter of India's greatest expert on the Asian elephant, the late Prince of Gauripur, who taught her everything. Shand sought out Parbati to take part in a film about the plight of the wild herds today in north-east India.

## THE DARKENING LEAF
### Caroline Stickland

On storm-tossed Chesil Bank in 1847, the young lovers, Philobeth and Frederick, prevent wreckers mutilating the apparent corpse of a young woman. Discovering she is still alive, Frederick takes her to his grandmother's home. But the rescue is to have violent and far-reaching effects . . .

## A WOMAN'S TOUCH
### Emma Stirling

When Fenn went to stay on her uncle's farm in Africa, the lovely Helena Starr seemed to resent her — especially when Dr Jason Kemp agreed to Fenn helping in his bush hospital. Though it seemed Jason saw Fenn as little more than a child, her feelings for him were those of a woman.

## A DEAD GIVEAWAY
### Various Authors

This book offers the perfect opportunity to sample the skills of five of the finest writers of crime fiction — Clare Curzon, Gillian Linscott, Peter Lovesey, Dorothy Simpson and Margaret Yorke.